Six more military heroes.
Six more indomitable heroines.
One *Uniformly Hot!* miniseries.

Don't miss a story in Harlequin Blaze's bestselling miniseries, featuring irresistible soldiers from all branches of the armed forces.

Catch Chance's thrilling story in

Coming Up for Air
by Karen Foley
(May 2012)

and his twin brother Chase's sexy adventure in

No Going Back
by Karen Foley
(July 2012)

Uniformly Hot!
The Few. The Proud. The Sexy as Hell.

Blaze

Dear Reader,

I have a military friend who is deployed somewhere in Afghanistan, and one of his duties is to escort visiting celebrities. As he says, it's tough duty but someone has to do it! But it got me wondering what might happen if a bad-ass covert ops specialist was directed to escort a pampered celebrity—and her bossy, overprotective publicist—on an Independence Day tour of Afghanistan?

I first introduced Major Chase Rawlins to readers in my May book, *Coming Up for Air*. Although he and his brother are identical twins, they couldn't be more different. As a member of the Army's elite special ops, Chase is all business, all the time. So when he's assigned to keep tabs on prickly publicist Kate Fitzgerald, he's determined to keep it strictly professional. But soon Kate is placing herself in his capable hands at every opportunity, and he finds that even hardened soldiers have their weaknesses.

I love writing about strong, sexy military heroes and the women who bring them to their knees. I hope you enjoy Chase and Kate's story!

Happy reading,

Karen

Karen Foley

NO GOING BACK

HARLEQUIN®
entertain, enrich, inspire™

ISBN-13: 978-0-373-79702-8

NO GOING BACK

This is a work of fiction. Names, characters, places and incidents are either the product of the author's imagination or are used fictitiously, and any resemblance to actual persons, living or dead, business establishments, events or locales is entirely coincidental.

This edition published by arrangement with Harlequin Books S.A.

For questions and comments about the quality of this book please contact us at Customer_eCare@Harlequin.ca.

® and TM are trademarks of Harlequin Enterprises Limited or its corporate affiliates. Trademarks indicated with ® are registered in the United States Patent and Trademark Office, the Canadian Trade Marks Office and in other countries.

www.Harlequin.com

Printed in U.S.A.

ABOUT THE AUTHOR

Karen Foley is an incurable romantic. When she's not working for the Department of Defense, she's writing sexy romances with strong heroes and happy endings. She lives in Massachusetts with her husband and two daughters, an overgrown puppy and two very spoiled cats. Karen enjoys hearing from her readers. You can find out more about her by visiting www.karenefoley.com.

Books by Karen Foley

HARLEQUIN BLAZE
353—FLYBOY
422—OVERNIGHT SENSATION
451—ABLE-BODIED
504—HOLD ON TO THE NIGHTS
549—BORN ON THE 4TH OF JULY
    "Packing Heat"
563—HOT-BLOODED
596—HEAT OF THE MOMENT
640—DEVIL IN DRESS BLUES
682—COMING UP FOR AIR

To get the inside scoop on Harlequin Blaze and its talented writers, be sure to check out blazeauthors.com.

All backlist available in ebook. Don't miss any of our special offers. Write to us at the following address for information on our newest releases.

Harlequin Reader Service
U.S.: 3010 Walden Ave., P.O. Box 1325, Buffalo, NY 14269
Canadian: P.O. Box 609, Fort Erie, Ont. L2A 5X3

This book is dedicated to our men and women
in uniform; thank you for your service!

1

An imperious knocking on the door of the opulent hotel suite startled Kate Fitzgerald from her disturbing thoughts. Hurrying to the door, she peered through the peephole and then opened it wide to the man who stalked inside, dragging his hand through his long hair.

"Keep your voice down," she said without preamble, closing the door behind him. "Tenley is sleeping in the next room."

Russell Wilson might look like a British rock star with his skinny jeans, necklaces and leather jacket, but he was one of the most coveted talent agents in the country. Kate could see he was angry, and she couldn't blame him.

"The video of Tenley's meltdown has gone viral," he snapped. "It's only been three days, and every social media and video-sharing website is promoting it. Even the major news networks have picked it up. Bloody hell, what a train wreck."

Kate chewed the edge of her thumb as she watched him pace. Behind her on the flat-screen television, the evening news was running yet another clip of Tenley Miles's anti-military rant, caught by several fans on their cell phones and provided to the media. Kate cringed as she listened to Tenley

scream about how the military was medieval in its enlist-
ment tactics, brutal in its treatment of new recruits and uncaring of the young men and women who gave their lives to
feed its ravenous appetite. But worst of all, she'd concluded
her shocking meltdown by stating she was ashamed to call
herself an American. Was Tenley overdramatic? Certainly.
But even knowing her sister's tendency toward extreme emo-
tions, Kate had to admit it looked bad.

"I'm more concerned about Tenley than I am about her
fans," Kate said. "She's emotionally fragile right now."

Russell gave a snort. "When isn't she emotionally fragile?
Whatever possessed her to run off with a complete stranger
and get *married* is beyond me. At least you had the good
sense to have it annulled."

Kate sighed and moved to the window to gaze out at the
lights of San Antonio. Tenley would perform at the AT&T
Center later that night before heading to Dallas for two
shows, and then finally home to Nashville. Had it really
been only a week since they'd spent three nights in Las
Vegas? Since her sister had met Corporal Doug Armstrong,
a young soldier who had scored backstage tickets to meet
her, and had run off with him? She'd hated hurting Tenley
by using her role as legal guardian to have the marriage annulled, but she wouldn't let anyone take advantage of her
sister's soft heart—or her substantial bank account—no
matter how handsome or charming he might be.

"I didn't have a choice," she said tonelessly, staring
through the glass at the neon lights of the strip below. "They
barely knew each other, and he's stationed in California.
What did she think—that she and Doug were going to move
there and they would live happily ever after?"

Kate closed her eyes against the memory of Tenley telling her she had just gotten married, and her own reaction to
the news. If it had been anyone else, Kate might have been

inclined to let the newlyweds discover for themselves that they'd made a terrible mistake. But a failed marriage would destroy Tenley, and if they were to have a child…

No, she'd made the right decision. The annulment might cause Tenley pain now, but that pain would be far worse if Kate had allowed the marriage to continue. She only hoped her sister would forgive her for interfering.

"Well, so long as the public doesn't learn about the elopement, then no harm done," Russell finally said. "Although it will be hard to keep the information quiet after that public display. People will want to know what caused her to act so out of character, and we can hardly tell them her bitterness toward the military is because her husband—to whom, by the way, she is no longer married—has just been shipped off to Afghanistan for a year." Russell gave Kate a smile. "That was a great move, by the way."

Kate compressed her lips but didn't immediately say anything. If Tenley ever discovered that Kate was the one responsible for having the young man peremptorily shipped overseas, she'd never forgive her. All it had taken was a couple of phone calls, and the deed was done. Kate didn't regret her actions. She had acted in Tenley's best interests.

As the daughter of two famous singers, both of whom had been killed in a bus accident when she was just a child, Tenley Miles was the darling of the country-music scene. She'd grown up in the public spotlight and her sweet disposition and naivety, combined with the obstacles she had overcome, had helped to fuel her popularity.

Kate still remembered the day she had gotten the news that their mother and her fiancé had been killed. She'd been just two months into her freshman year of college and the news had changed her life forever. She'd wanted to become part of the exploding internet industry and had been excited about the prospect of designing programs that would connect people with others around the globe. But when she learned that her mother had died, she'd left college to care for her then six-year-old sister. That had been twelve years ago. She didn't regret her decision, and if her own dreams of becoming a web designer weren't progressing as quickly as she'd hoped, then she had only herself to blame. She'd made her choice and she told herself that she didn't regret any of it. Besides, she'd been able to help Tenley achieve her own success.

At just eighteen years old, Tenley Miles was the biggest thing to hit the country pop scene in more than three years. She'd signed her first recording contract at just fifteen years old, and her debut single had spent eight weeks in the number-one spot on the country charts. A year later, she had released two albums and won five Grammys, along with a dozen other awards. By the time she was seventeen, she was filling music halls and stadiums around the country and each of her four albums had gone platinum. Her anti-military rant could definitely have a negative impact on her image, especially if the news got out about her elopement with a soldier. The last thing Kate needed was for Russell to drop his young client just when the country singer's career was skyrocketing.

"Look, I'll do damage control, I promise," Kate said to Russell. "We'll figure this out."

Russell whirled on her in disbelief, his eyebrows nearly disappearing into his hairline. "Damage control? Are you freaking joking?" He gave a laugh of disbelief. "Katie, darling, do you realize her little diatribe cost her nearly half of her audience attendance at last night's concert? Her recording label called this morning to say that she's already receiving hate mail. They can't afford this kind of negative publicity and are actually considering dropping her. What kind of damage control can you possibly do after *that?*" He stabbed his finger in the direction of the television, where a fan had caught the country pop star having her very public, very ugly meltdown. "It's bad enough that she eloped during a concert tour with some soldier, but now this? It's like she's deliberately trying to sabotage her own career."

Kate bit her tongue and forced herself to remain calm. "You know Tenley," she replied. "She's impulsive. That's why she has me."

"And what are you going to do about this?" Russell snapped in irritation. "In less than five minutes that girl has managed to destroy everything we've worked so hard to create. She's alienated every patriotic and uniformed person in this country. Christ, there's a public outcry to boycott her music. Even the liberals are lambasting her."

"Keep your voice down," Kate admonished, glancing toward the bedroom door. "I have an idea, one that will demonstrate her goodwill toward the troops."

"It had better be good," Russell snarled. "If she has to cancel the rest of her tour—which is looking more likely with every passing hour—this is going to get very expensive, very quickly."

Kate pulled her cell phone out of her pocket and began scrolling through her extensive list of contacts. "I've been thinking about the huge Independence Day concert tour taking place in Afghanistan next month," she said, slanting Russell a quick look. "Everyone is talking about it. In fact, I believe several of your biggest clients are participating. Let me make a few calls and see if we can squeeze Tenley into the lineup."

"You can't be serious," Russell groaned. "Do you know the hoops I had to jump through to get my other clients on that tour? Even if you could pull it off, it's too late! Tenley can't just cancel her scheduled performances to go overseas."

Kate arched an eyebrow. "To hear you tell it, she'll be

lucky if her remaining performances aren't canceled due to lack of interest. But I'm not buying it. Tenley is a box-office juggernaut, and I can't imagine that the USO won't be thrilled to have her join the tour."

"And what makes you think Tenley will agree to go over there?"

Kate gave a tight smile. "Are you kidding? She'll jump at the opportunity to be in the same country as her lost love, even for just a few days. Not that there'll be any chance of seeing him, of course. My understanding is that he was sent to one of the remote outposts in the northern part of the country."

Russell was silent for a moment as he considered Kate's words. "That might just work," he mused. "Of course, the USO may not agree to finance her trip, especially at this late date, so we could have to pay for it out of pocket. That's disappointing, but if it works…"

"I'll make it work," Kate promised.

Russell raised his eyebrows. "You've always been so protective of Tenley. Are you sure you want to send her to a combat zone?"

Kate gave him a tolerant look. "If Carrie Underwood and Faith Hill can do the tour, then so can Tenley. It's not as if she won't have ample protection. Besides, I'd rather send her to Afghanistan for a week than see her career crash and burn."

Glancing toward the bedroom door, Russell lowered his voice. "I've always thought you were too easy on her, and I'm glad to see you finally take off the kid gloves."

Kate looked at him in exasperation. "I'm not doing this to punish her. I'm doing it because I care about her. After all, she's my baby sister."

"Half sister," he corrected.

"The point is," Kate said carefully, "I'm all she has. Nobody else is going to look out for her, and she's certainly not capable of looking out for herself. The fact that she ran off with the first guy she met is proof of that. She *needs* me."

"Hmm," mused Russell. "Still, it *is* Afghanistan."

"This is a huge Independence Day event," Kate said. "Trust me, if there was any danger, the USO wouldn't allow the concert to proceed. In fact, my plan is to arrive a few days ahead of Tenley, tour the various bases where the concerts will take place, and ensure the proper security measures are set up." She smiled at Russell. "She'll have the entire United States Army to protect her. What could possibly go wrong?"

2

Bagram Airfield, Afghanistan

"WHAT DO YOU MEAN we've been told to stand down?" Chase Rawlins growled at the uniformed man standing behind the desk.

Colonel Decker planted his hands on the surface of the desk and leaned forward. When he spoke, his voice was hard. "Major, we've known each other for a long time, but I'll advise you not to forget who you're speaking to."

Chase stared at the other man for a long moment, trying to rein in his frustration. Compressing his lips, he straightened and stared at a point over the colonel's shoulder. "Yes, sir."

He and his men had been in the middle of a critical operation when the stand-down order had come through. The team of special-operations commandos had been relentlessly tracking a top Taliban leader through northern Afghanistan for nearly a year. They had finally discovered him hiding out in a heavily fortified village in the mountains, and had been preparing a nighttime raid to capture him, when they had received the order to stand down and return to Bagram Airfield.

Immediately.

He and his men had literally been positioned on the bastard's doorstep. Chase had reluctantly acknowledged the order and signaled his team to retreat. The fact that one of his men had chosen to disregard that order and had attempted to singlehandedly storm the compound where the target was hiding was proof of the sheer frustration they all felt. Chase had managed to stop the soldier before he actually gained entry to the building, but not before their position had been compromised. The ensuing firefight was intense, but Chase's team had escaped to the west and made their way to the extraction point, where a Black Hawk helicopter had picked them up and returned them to Bagram Airfield. Two members of his team had stayed behind to maintain surveillance on the target.

But the knowledge that they'd let Hamid Al-Azir get away pissed him off on a level so deep that he hadn't stopped to fully consider his actions. As soon as the helicopter had touched down at Bagram, he'd stormed over to the Special Ops commander's office to find out what the hell was going on. He hadn't even stopped to clean himself up and still wore the dust and grime of fourteen days in the field.

"I understand your frustration, Major," Colonel Decker said. "Vital operations have been disrupted across the theater, but the Pentagon has demanded a full investigation into the U.S. air strike that occurred outside Kandahar two days ago. Until that investigation is complete, your orders are to stand down."

Chase hadn't read the reports, but by all accounts the Special Ops air strike against the summer retreat of a top Taliban leader had been a complete disaster. The local population claimed that dozens of innocent civilians had been targeted, and Washington's response was an abrupt and complete halt to all special-operations missions.

Chase blew out a hard breath and looked at Colonel Decker. "How long?"

The Colonel shrugged. "The Pentagon says at least forty-eight hours, but my guess is a week. Maybe longer."

Chase bit back an expletive. At least with a two-man team in the region, they could still keep tabs on Al-Azir. The months spent tracking the Taliban leader wouldn't be completely wasted, but Chase didn't think he could relax until they had the bastard in custody.

"Sir, I'd like to rejoin my surveillance team ASAP."

Colonel Decker picked up a folder and pinioned Chase with a hard look. "Before I let you do that, why don't you tell me what happened after the stand-down order was issued? My report states gunfire was exchanged at the compound, and your team requested air support."

The Colonel's expression was grim and Chase knew it didn't bode well for him. "Sergeant Morse was unaware of the stand-down order," he lied, "and attempted to take the target into custody."

"Uh-huh." The dry tone clearly said the Colonel didn't believe a word of Chase's story. "And as their leader, your responsibility was to ensure your men not only heard the order, but heeded it."

"Yes, sir."

"In light of your inability to control your team, Major, I have a new assignment for you. Here, take a look. This should keep you busy for the next week or so. How well you perform this duty will determine whether I send you back into the field."

Frowning, Chase took the file from his superior and opened it, quickly scanning the contents of the dossier. Along with the usual personal information, the folder contained several glossy media photos of a young woman with a guitar. She was attractive in a sexy, teenybopper way, with wild blond hair and heavy eye makeup. She wore a pair of tattered jeans and cowboy boots, paired with a red camisole top that laced up the front like a corset. Scanning the dossier, he saw her name was Tenley Miles and she was some kind of country-pop singer. And she was coming to Afghanistan.

"What is this?" he growled, but he had a sinking suspicion that he already knew.

"Your new assignment," Colonel Decker announced cheerfully. "She'll arrive in three days as part of the Independence Day concert tour, and you will act as her escort while she's here."

"Her babysitter, you mean," Chase muttered, flipping through the photos. A quick appraisal of her personal information confirmed that she was barely eighteen years old. "Why isn't the USO handling security? This isn't something we do."

While Chase and his men routinely provided protection details for VIPs and dignitaries during their visits to Afghanistan, they had never been asked to act as bodyguards to celebrities. The USO had its own contracted security personnel for that purpose.

"The USO staff is stretched thin with the other entertainers who are coming over. Besides, she's not here on a USO ticket," the colonel added. "She's here on her own dime to make nice with the troops and, as I understand it, try to repair the damage she did at a recent concert when she publicly lambasted the U.S. military."

"Christ, leave it to the celebrities," Chase said in disgust. He pulled out a news article that provided the details of Tenley Miles's anti-military rant. He gave a disbelieving huff of laughter as he quickly read the column. "I think I'd rather take my chances with the Taliban."

"Are you telling me you can't handle one girl?" The colonel arched an eyebrow.

"That depends," Chase said absently, thumbing through the remaining documents. "Is water-boarding still allowed?" Picking up a black-and-white photo, he studied it for a moment before turning it toward the other man. "Who is this?"

"Her personal assistant."

There was some writing on the back of the photo. "Katherine Fitzgerald," Chase read aloud. "Publicist." He gave a snort of disgust. "Great. Tell me I don't have to babysit her as well."

Turning the photo over, he studied the woman again and something fisted low in his gut. She was slender and her face boasted beautiful bone structure, although her baggy cargo pants and cardigan sweater effectively hid any curves she might have. Her hair was an indeterminate color and style, having been pulled back into a ponytail. Her eyes were hidden behind a pair of sunglasses, and Chase let his gaze linger for a moment on her full lips and the determined set of her chin.

"Actually," the colonel said, "her flight lands in about two hours and I'd like you to be there to meet her and get her settled."

Chase frowned. The last thing he wanted to do was pander to some entitled celebrity and her publicist. "I thought you said she wasn't coming for another three days."

"Tenley Miles won't be here for another three days," the Colonel clarified. "Her publicist arrives today to scope things out. So...you have three days to tour three of our bases—Bagram, Camp Leatherneck and Kandahar, where you'll rendezvous with the entertainers upon their arrival."

Chase frowned. "Is that typical protocol for these kinds of events? To send a publicist or personal assistant—or whatever the hell she calls herself—over early to scope things out?"

"I guess that depends on the star power of the celebrity,"

Colonel Decker said wryly. "And I'm not into the country-pop scene, but my understanding is that Tenley Miles is a very big deal."

"So if the USO has run out of room, where am I supposed to put her?"

"I'll leave that up to you. But keep in mind that how well you perform this assignment will determine how quickly I allow you to return to the field with the rest of your team."

In other words, if he couldn't handle these two women, there was no way he'd be allowed to oversee a covert Special Ops team.

"Just so that I'm clear," he said carefully, "I have complete responsibility for this woman while she's here, correct?"

"That's right."

"And if she's not happy with the, uh, accommodations?"

"Then she goes home. Same thing for the singer. I won't compromise their safety or the safety of the troops, so if either of them is unable to follow your rules, Major, then they're on the next flight out. But you won't let that happen. They *will* follow your rules, do we understand each other?"

Chase read the unspoken message loud and clear. If the women ended up leaving early, it would only be because he had failed in his assignment. And if that happened, he could expect to spend the remainder of his deployment chained to a desk somewhere. He considered the factors involved in the first phase of his assignment: one woman, three bases, three days. No problem. He hadn't failed a mission yet, and he wasn't about to start now.

KATE DECIDED THAT planning a trip to Afghanistan was a little like planning a trip to the moon. She had no idea what to expect and, therefore, little idea what to bring. In the end, she'd packed lightweight, practical clothing. She still believed that allowing Tenley to visit the troops in Afghanistan was the right thing to do, although seeing all the uniformed soldiers on the last leg of her trip had admittedly given her pause. They'd both be lucky if they didn't get themselves killed, and after Tenley's public meltdown, Kate thought they were probably in as much danger from the troops as they were from terrorists.

She had known it would take a long time to reach her destination, but she'd been unprepared for just how exhausted she'd be when she finally reached Bagram Airfield, more than forty-eight hours after leaving Nashville. Additionally, since she had been forced to make her own travel arrangements, there hadn't been anyone to meet her at each location and direct her where to go next. At least when she traveled with Tenley, they had Russell to lean on. But after assuring Kate that she'd do splendidly on her own, he'd left her at the airport. Even Tenley hadn't been overly interested in any of the travel plans, although she'd perked up a bit when Kate had told her they would be going to Afghanistan. But after breaking the news that there would be absolutely no likelihood of seeing her young soldier, Tenley had retreated to her bedroom in tears, preferring to be alone until she received word from Kate that she'd okayed the security setup and Tenley could fly over. For the first time Kate could recall, she was traveling completely alone.

She'd arrived in Kuwait the previous afternoon and had waited nearly fourteen hours for a military flight to Bagram Airfield. Now she watched as the base came into view on the ground below. From a distance, the place looked enormous, but for as far as she could see there were only unrelenting shades of brown, from the desert to the distant mountains, and even the base itself. Opening her shoulder bag, Kate looked again at the information that the Army Morale, Welfare and Recreation department had sent to her.

Over the course of a week, Tenley would perform concerts at three different American bases in Afghanistan, as well as conduct meet-and-greet sessions with the troops. The USO had assured Kate that someone would meet her upon her arrival, and escort her to each location. Kate had spent most of the flight writing Tenley's speech, in which her sister apologized for her thoughtless rant and pledged her support for the men and women in uniform. Kate only hoped it would be enough.

The big jet touched down on the airstrip at Bagram Airfield, and Kate was surprised to see they would disembark directly onto the tarmac. Peering out the window of the plane, she couldn't see any building that looked remotely like an airport terminal. The airfield seemed to be nothing more than an enormous airstrip alongside a cluster of tents and makeshift hangars, and a hodgepodge of other small buildings. Maybe this wasn't the airfield at all. Maybe the plane was making an unscheduled stop at some remote base and then they would head on to Bagram.

The aisle of the plane was quickly filling with uniformed soldiers waiting to disembark. Leaning forward, Kate tugged on the sleeve of the nearest man. He turned and looked at her expectantly.

"Excuse me, but is this Bagram Field?"

"Yes, ma'am."

"Are you sure? I mean, have you been here before?"

"Yes, ma'am," he assured her. "This is my third deployment."

"Oh. Well, where exactly is the terminal? I mean, where do I pick up my luggage?"

Ducking his head to avoid the overhead storage bins, the soldier leaned across the seat and pointed through the window. "See that hangar, there? That's the terminal. This is an airfield, ma'am, as in air*field*. They're not really set up like you're used to at home. Look, they're bringing the luggage out now."

Kate watched as a group of soldiers began systematically dragging baggage from the cargo hold of the plane, only instead of stacking the items on a small trolley to be transported into the terminal, they literally threw the bags into one enormous pile right there on the flight line. When the mountain of duffel bags threatened to fall over, they started a new pile right next to it.

"Oh, my God," she breathed. "How am I supposed to find my bag?"

The soldier gave her a grin and straightened. "Well, ma'am, that's half the fun. Welcome to Afghanistan, and good luck."

Kate watched helplessly as he departed, then scooped her shoulder bag up and fell into line behind the soldiers. As soon as she stepped out the door of the aircraft, the heat slapped her in the face like a hot brick. To compound the discomfort, the air itself was filled with a fine, powdery dust that immediately infiltrated her mouth and nose and sent her into a fit of uncontrollable sneezing.

"Oh, my God," she gasped, when she could finally catch her breath.

The soldier in front of her turned around and gave her a quick grin. "You'll get used it."

Kate doubted it. She'd never experienced heat like this. It seemed to suck the very moisture out of her skin and left her gasping for breath. Even Las Vegas in the summer hadn't been this oppressive. At the bottom of the airplane steps, she automatically turned toward the piles of luggage, but found her way blocked by a military police officer.

"Just follow the line for processing, ma'am," he said briskly, indicating she should continue toward the nearest hangar. "You'll be notified when all the baggage is out of the aircraft."

In dismay, Kate saw that the line snaked across the tarmac and disappeared inside one of the makeshift hangars. It was moving at a snail's pace, and Kate knew she would die of heat stroke before she ever made it into the building. She could almost feel the sweat evaporating from her skin as she stood under the baking sun.

Hefting her shoulder bag higher, she looked around her, astonished at the sheer number of men. There were men *everywhere*—soldiers who seemed to be waiting for transportation, soldiers sleeping or sitting upright against their gear, soldiers reading books, standing around in small groups, playing handheld video games or listening to music on their ear buds. There was a handful of female soldiers, but they were hugely outnumbered by the men. Kate couldn't help but notice that all of them—male and female—carried some sort of weapon.

She was acutely conscious of her own vulnerability. She carried no weapon, unless you counted the Montegrappa pen that Tenley had brought back from Italy as a gift for her. She didn't even possess a helmet or bulletproof vest. Who would protect her in the event of an attack?

"Miss Fitzgerald?"

Kate turned to see a soldier striding toward her—a tall, muscular soldier who looked like he kicked ass for a living. He had the easy, loose-limbed gait of an athlete, and as he drew closer, Kate swallowed hard. The growth of beard he sported couldn't hide his square jaw or detract from the chiseled cheekbones and proud nose. With his broad shoulders and powerful arms, he looked more than a little dangerous. The thought flashed through her head that given a few spare hours, this guy could singlehandedly end the war.

"Yes?" Her hand went self-consciously to her hair, and she tried to ignore the way her pulse kicked up a notch.

As he came forward, he yanked his sunglasses off and she saw his eyes were a translucent green, startling in his tanned face. Her breath caught and she found herself helpless to look away. He was the stuff of heroic action movies, a combination of masculine strength and confidence all wrapped up in a mouthwatering package. She'd never had this kind of immediate reaction to a man before. Her heart raced, and her knees were actually wobbly. Feeling a little panicked, Kate tried to recall the last time she'd eaten. Her blood sugar must be low. Either that or she was dehydrated.

The soldier extended his hand and his eyes swept over her in sharp assessment. "Ma'am. I'm Major Rawlins. I'll be your military escort for the duration of your visit."

His hand gripped hers, and she barely had time to register how warm and callused his palm was against her own before he released her.

"If you'll follow me, please."

Without giving her an opportunity to respond and without waiting to see if she would do as he said, he turned and walked toward the hangar. Kate watched his retreating back, feeling as if she'd had the wind knocked out of her. Then, realizing her mouth was hanging open, she snapped it shut and stepped out of the line to hurry after him, her oversize shoulder bag bouncing uncomfortably against her hip.

"Major Rawlins," she called as she caught up with him.

He glanced over at her but did not slow down. "Yes?"

"My understanding was that the USO would provide a civilian representative who would be my point of contact." As he strode briskly along, Kate tried to simultaneously walk and fish through her bag for the paperwork she had received from the USO, but the task was nearly impossible given the pace he set. Maybe she'd misunderstood him.

Maybe he was only her driver. Oh, God, please let him be the driver. She'd never felt so self-conscious or tongue-tied as she did with this guy, evidence that she'd gone too long without male contact. Or at least, gorgeous male contact.

"You understood wrong, ma'am," he said smoothly, never breaking stride.

Abandoning the search for her papers, Kate concentrated instead on keeping up with him. Arriving at the front of the long line, she saw several military police scanning everyone's identification cards. Flashing his own ID, Major Rawlins stepped into the front of the line and looked expectantly at Kate.

"You should have been assigned a temporary identification card when you arrived at the processing center in Kuwait," he explained carefully. "Do you have it with you?"

"What? Oh, yes!" Setting her bag down on the table, Kate began rummaging through it. She'd purchased a bright orange lanyard for the card, specifically so she could locate it in a hurry, but with everything else she'd managed to stuff into the large tote, she couldn't locate the identification.

"Sorry," she mumbled, uncomfortably aware of Major Rawlins's growing irritation. "I know it's in here somewhere."

Pulling out two paperback novels, an MP3 player and a bag of trail mix, she set them on the table and continued digging through the contents of the bag. Behind her, she heard several soldiers mutter something under their breath and knew she was holding up the line. She glanced at the military police officer who watched her impassively with his arms crossed over his chest.

"Sorry," she muttered again.

"Here, let me help you," Major Rawlins offered.

Kate thought she saw the hint of a dimple in one lean cheek, and before she could protest, he took her bag and upended it, spilling the contents onto the table. Ignoring Kate's gasp, he swept one finger through the assorted flotsam and came up with the ID card attached to the orange lanyard. Yanking the card from the holder, he handed it to the military police officer.

"You see? That wasn't so difficult," he said, amusement lacing his voice. Accepting the ID card back from the officer, he returned it to Kate. "Wear this where it's visible. Follow me, please."

Dropping the lanyard over her head, Kate watched with rising annoyance as he made his way back toward the flight line. With one hand, she swept her personal items back into her shoulder bag and determinedly followed Major Rawlins.

"Find your gear and let's go," he said, nodding toward the three enormous piles of duffel bags sitting on the tarmac.

Kate glanced at his face to see if he was joking. With his sunglasses shielding his eyes, she couldn't decipher his expression, but it seemed he had no intention of helping her. Glancing at the daunting piles, she drew in a deep breath.

"Here, hold this," she said, and pushed her shoulder bag into his hands. She sensed his surprise, but he made no objection, tucking the bag under his arm as he watched her.

Kate had packed her belongings in a neon-pink duffel bag that had once belonged to Tenley, thinking it would be easy to spot. But she'd been wrong. Circling each of the piles, she couldn't see any sign of pink peeking through the dozens of army-green duffel bags, which meant her own was probably buried somewhere near the bottom. She prepared to grab the handles of the nearest duffel when a masculine voice interrupted her.

"Ma'am, are you looking for a particular bag?"

Turning, she saw two young soldiers walking toward her. Just moments earlier, they had been lounging against their own piles of gear, chatting idly.

Kate nodded. "Yes. I have a bright pink duffel bag, but I can't see it anywhere."

The second soldier, who looked to be no older than Tenley, grinned. "No problem, ma'am, we can find it for you." Turning, he whistled through his teeth to a group of soldiers gathered near the entrance to the hangar and motioned them over. "Hey, guys, give us a hand over here!"

Within minutes, there were a dozen young men enthusiastically digging their way through the piles of luggage, calling out names as they identified a tag or lettering painted on the outside of the bag. Kate stepped back to watch, amazed by their enthusiasm and efficiency. In less than five minutes, the first soldier held Kate's bag up in triumph.

"Is this it?" he asked.

Kate came forward and took the duffel from him. "That's the one," she said with a grateful smile. "Thank you so much!"

"My pleasure, ma'am."

Clutching the heavy bag, Kate turned back to Major Rawlins, who stood to one side with his arms crossed over his impressive chest, her tote dangling from one hand. She wasn't certain, but Kate thought she detected amusement on his face.

"Well, that wasn't so bad," she remarked cheerfully.

He raised an eyebrow and gave a noncommittal grunt. "Here, let's trade," he said, handing her the shoulder bag and taking the pink duffel from her. "I have a vehicle waiting out front."

Kate watched as he walked back toward the hangar, a tough-as-nails warrior carrying a pink duffel bag in his hand. She wanted to laugh at the incongruous sight, but seeing that none of the surrounding soldiers so much as cracked a smile in his direction, she suppressed her own amusement. Drawing herself up, she followed him once more. She was getting tired of seeing nothing but this man's backside, no matter how delectable it might be. And she had to admit, he did have a fine ass. Frowning at her thoughts, she hefted her tote bag over her shoulder and followed him.

"Major Rawlins, I'd like to get started right away," she said, trying to match his long strides. "I understand that with the sheer number of entertainers who are coming over, the USO ran out of room to accommodate my client and her band. I'd like to see where Tenley will stay while she's here. And do you know who will accompany me to the other bases?"

He did stop then, so abruptly that Kate nearly plowed into him. Slowly, he removed his sunglasses and turned to face her. His gaze drifted over her and that muscle worked in his lean cheek. Kate felt herself go hot beneath his regard, and she wondered what was going through his head.

"Just so that we're clear," he said carefully, "I am your single point of contact for whatever you require while you are here. We will travel together, eat together, view the venues together and basically be attached at the hip until you depart. This is a combat environment, Miss Fitzgerald, and I'm responsible for your well-being. You don't do anything without me, or without my permission. Understood?"

Kate stared at him, and for the first time since she'd made the decision to come to Afghanistan, realized the personal impact. The knowledge that she would spend the next three days in this man's exclusive company caused a shiver to go through her, but whether it was one of dread or anticipation, she couldn't tell.

Major Rawlins was unlike any man she'd ever met before. He was testosterone personified, and the way he looked at her made her go a little boneless. For the first time she could recall, she wasn't the one in control, the one calling the shots. That fact should have annoyed her. Instead, she found herself agreeing wholeheartedly to his conditions.

"Yes." She nodded. "I understand."

She thought he would turn and walk away again, but he stood watching for a moment longer, as if there was something about her that puzzled him. His eyes were a gorgeous shade of green, reminding her of the clear, warm waters of the Caribbean.

"I'm curious. Why are you here, Miss Fitzgerald?"

She frowned, taken aback by the question. "I beg your pardon? It's my job to ensure everything is ready for my client's visit."

"But why are you *here?* In Afghanistan? Why not some military base on American soil? Why come all the way over here when your client wasn't originally scheduled to perform as part of the Independence Day concert?" He rubbed the back of his neck. "No offense, but Tenley Miles is little more than a child, and you—" He broke abruptly off.

"What?" Kate asked. "I'm what?"

He gave a soft laugh. "Well, I just can't figure out why a woman like you would come over here, unaccompanied."

Kate hesitated. She had to assume that he knew the truth; that he'd seen the news reports and was aware that Tenley had directed her vitriol toward the military's policy of sending troops to Iraq and Afghanistan. She couldn't blame him for his attitude, but neither could she explain to him the reasons behind Tenley's meltdown. Her sister's precipitous marriage and subsequent annulment had to remain a secret.

She hesitated, wondering how direct she could be without giving him too much information. "Tenley has been going through a difficult time," she began cautiously. "She said some things about the military that were pretty horrible and, well…" She gave a soft laugh. "Let's just say that I'm hoping this tour will be a humbling experience for her."

"Oh, I'm certain it will be," he said, and one corner of his mouth lifted in a ghost of a smile. He glanced at his watch. "We should get going."

Outside, the unrelenting heat, combined with the weight of her overloaded tote bag, quickly sapped her strength. She felt tired and achy and unprepared for whatever lay ahead. A military Humvee waited by the curb, and Kate watched as Major Rawlins put her gear in the back.

"Thank you," she murmured as he held the door open for her. Climbing into the vehicle, she saw there was already another soldier behind the wheel. She expected Major Rawlins to get in the front passenger seat, and was unprepared when he slid in beside her, instead.

Sensing her surprise, he gave her a wry smile. "Attached at the hip, remember?"

Kate found herself staring at him. That small smile was enough to transform his features. How would he look if that smile were to expand to his eyes? She had a feeling that he might be irresistible.

"Where to, sir?" asked the driver.

"Take us to my housing unit."

"Yes sir." The driver grinned. "I know one female who is going to be very excited to see you again."

Kate slanted Major Rawlins a questioning look, but if he felt her silent query, he ignored it. She felt a tug of curiosity. What would it be like to be romantically involved with this man? To have his whole and undivided attention? To see his eyes go hot with desire? The thought sent a small shiver through her, further proof that she'd been way too long without sex. Men didn't usually have this effect on her, but having gone more than a year without intimacy of any kind, she suspected her hormones were on full alert and ready to revolt if she didn't do something soon to appease them. But this wasn't quite what she had in mind.

"Why are we going to your housing unit?" she asked. "Don't you think you're taking this attached-at-the-hip thing a little too seriously? I am not staying in your unit with you."

She watched, entranced, as a smile spread across his face. She'd been wrong. He wasn't just irresistible, he was downright devastating. His smile caused something to loosen inside her, and she found she couldn't look away.

"Miss Fitzgerald," he drawled, letting his gaze drift deliberately over her, "as attractive as you might be, I have no intention of sleeping with you."

3

CHASE REGRETTED THE WORDS the instant they left his mouth. Their driver gave a snort of laughter which he quickly hid behind a sudden coughing fit after Chase sent him a quelling look. But it was the stricken expression on Kate Fitzgerald's face that made him wish he'd kept his mouth shut. That, and the fact that a part of him recognized that given a different set of circumstances, she was the kind of woman he'd give his left nut to sleep with.

He wished like hell that she wasn't so damned pretty. The instant he'd spotted her standing in the long line of uniformed soldiers, he'd felt as if someone had kicked him in the solar plexus.

He'd been in Afghanistan for six months, and he'd spent most of that time in the stark, forbidding mountains of the Kala Gush region, living and sleeping outside and enduring the harshest of conditions. Seeing Kate Fitzgerald had been an unexpected and potent reminder of everything he'd left behind, and for just an instant, his heart had ached with longing.

He'd had a tough time catching his breath and had to mentally shake himself in order to stop staring at her. She stuck out like an exotic bloom among a bed of weeds in her jewel-colored shirt, and the bright sun picked out the deep red lights in her silky dark hair. Without the heavy cardigan she'd worn in the photo, he could see she definitely had curves. Nice curves. Curves that begged to be touched. And he wasn't the only one who had noticed. Every guy within fifty yards had been eyeballing her and he couldn't blame them. She looked good enough to eat.

Then she'd turned and looked at him.

He'd expected her to have blue or even green eyes, but hers were coffee-brown fringed with dark lashes. As he'd drawn closer, he saw the splattering of freckles across her face, as if someone had flung flecks of gold paint at her. And her mouth…Christ, he found himself conjuring up decadent images of just what she could do with that mouth. Her lips were pillowy plump and pink and had opened on a soft "oh" of surprise when he'd called her name. She'd looked achingly feminine and completely out of place among the soldiers who surrounded her.

Now, as he saw her reaction to his words, he felt like a complete dick. He'd hurt her feelings. Her mouth opened, and for a moment she looked at him, appalled, before she snapped her jaw shut. Chase watched as a slow flush crept up her neck.

Why had he said that he had no intention of sleeping with her? Had it been to remind himself that she was off-limits? Or to ensure she disliked him enough that she'd want nothing to do with him? Because he knew that if she gave any indication that she found him attractive, he'd be toast. Everything about her appealed to him. He'd almost forgotten how good a woman could smell, or how smooth her skin could be. Looking at Kate, he wondered how her skin would feel under his fingertips. She had turned her face toward the window and the sunlight picked out the golden freckles on her cheeks and forehead. He wanted to trace them with a fingertip.

"Look," he finally said, "I'm sorry. That was a poor attempt at humor. I mean, obviously I have no intention of sleeping with you—" He broke off at her expression of disbelief, as if she was amazed he was still talking. Lord, he was making a mess of it. Biting back a curse, he scrubbed a hand across his face and turned to the driver. "Step on it, Cochran."

"Just so that we're clear, Major Rawlins," Kate said in a low voice as she sat stiffly beside him, "I'm here strictly to represent my client and ensure that everything is in order for her visit."

Chase nodded, feeling like an idiot. "I understand, Miss Fitzgerald."

She rolled her eyes. "And please stop calling me that. My name is Kate."

He nodded. He could have told her his first name, but that would have encouraged a familiarity he wasn't sure he was willing to move toward. This woman lived in a world so far removed from his that it might as well be in a different galaxy. She was the personal assistant to a superstar, and even if that star was on the verge of imploding, this woman—Kate—was accustomed to a world of bright lights and privilege, where her associations ensured a luxurious and pampered lifestyle. He, on the other hand, spent weeks at a time crawling through the desert and mountains, without so much as a change of clothing or a shave, in the company of men whose specialties were the stuff of nightmares. What could they possibly have in common?

The Humvee drew to a stop in front of a row of containerized housing units, or CHUs, which were nothing more than metal shipping containers outfitted for habitation. Since arriving at Bagram, Chase had barely had time to meet with

Colonel Decker and then drop his gear off at the command headquarters before he'd had to meet Kate's flight. He was in desperate need of a shower and a clean uniform.

"Wait here," he said brusquely. "I just need to grab a few things."

Inside the housing unit, the furnishings were Spartan. A small office took up the front part of the unit, with a desk, a chair and his computer equipment. The back part was where he slept on a narrow bed, with only a small wardrobe and a bedside table for furnishings. He didn't even have a private latrine, but instead showered in the communal bathrooms with the rest of the troops. Since there were no other empty CHUs near his own, he'd had to improvise in finding Miss Fitzgerald a place to sleep where he could be nearby in case she needed anything. She wasn't going to like the arrangements.

Grabbing a clean uniform and underclothes from a shelf, he shoved them into a backpack, intending to snatch a quick shower at the first opportunity. As he straightened, he caught sight of himself in the small mirror over the dresser and nearly groaned aloud. His beard was longer than he normally allowed it to grow, and his skin was burnt to a mahogany hue. He'd lost some weight while he'd been on assignment and his face was leaner and harder than usual. He looked every inch a mercenary, and it was a wonder to him that Kate Fitzgerald felt comfortable enough to follow him anywhere.

Returning to the Humvee, he saw she was holding a cell phone out the window, fruitlessly searching for a signal. Throwing his backpack alongside her duffel bag, he opened the door and prepared to climb in beside her.

"Give it up," he advised drily. "There's no service over here."

Drawing her arm back into the vehicle, she turned to him

in dismay. "But how am I supposed to communicate with my people? With Tenley?"

Before he could answer, two soldiers rounded the corner. One of them, Sergeant Mike Donahue, called out to Chase.

"Hey, welcome back." He shook Chase's hand. "Tough break about the stand-down order. Have you been over to see Charity yet?"

Chase glanced at Kate, seeing the open curiosity in her eyes. "Uh, no. We just got back a few hours ago and I haven't had time. But as soon as I finish up here, I'll go see her. How is she?"

Donahue shrugged. "She hasn't been the same since you left. She just mopes around waiting for you to come back. Man, she is going to flip when she sees you."

"Uh-huh. Well, thanks for keeping an eye on her. I'll be over as soon as I can."

"You bet."

Chase climbed in beside Kate, but didn't offer an explanation. He could see the speculation in her eyes and knew she thought he had a girlfriend. How would she react if he told her that Charity was a homeless dog he'd rescued from the streets? He and his men had been performing a house-to-house search in a small village when they'd come across a group of boys abusing the dog. Chase had intervened, but he knew that as soon as he and his men left, the boys would continue to torture the poor animal. She'd looked at him with such soulful eyes that he hadn't had the heart to leave her. That had been six months ago, and she'd been with him ever since. The K-9 unit kept an eye on her when he was gone and had been teaching her how to track, which she picked up quickly.

He turned toward Kate, who was still trying to find a signal on her cell phone. "Look, I have a satellite phone in my housing unit. You're welcome to use that."

"That's fine for right now, but what about when we leave here and go to the next base?"

Amusement curved his mouth. "You think we have no way to communicate with the States? I promise you that 'your people' are only a phone call away, and a phone will be made available to you whenever you wish."

She continued to look at him, expectation written all over her face. Chase gave an exaggerated sigh. "Fine. C'mon, you can make your call now."

Climbing out of the Humvee, he opened the door to his CHU and indicated she should precede him inside. As he dialed the code for outgoing calls, he watched her out of the corner of his eye. She was staring with interest and un-disguised dismay at his tiny rooms, even going so far as to peek into the bedroom at the rear. In the close quarters of the CHU, he could actually smell her fragrance, and his mind was immediately swamped with images of her spread across his narrow bed.

"Here," he said, holding out the receiver for her. "You can make your call."

She turned away from his bedroom and accepted the phone. He stood by her shoulder as she dialed the number, so close that he could see the tiny throb of her pulse along the side of her neck, and he had an almost overwhelming urge to bend his head and drag his mouth over the smooth skin.

Spinning away, he scrubbed a hand over his face. He was losing it. His only excuse was that he'd spent way too much time in the field, away from civilization. What other reason could there be for his unexpected reaction to her nearness?

"Tenley, it's me, Katie," he listened to her say. "If you're there, pick up please." She paused. "Okay, listen, there's no cell phone reception over here in Afghanistan, so you're not going to be able to call me." Putting her hand over the receiver, she looked at Chase. "What time can I call her back?"

Chase glanced at his watch. "It's four o'clock now, which means it's seven-thirty in the morning on the East Coast. What time would you like to call her back?"

"She's probably at the gym with her phone turned off. How does she expect anyone to reach her if she turns her phone off?" She blew out a hard breath and he watched as she pulled a small planner out of her shoulder bag and quickly flipped it open. As she scanned the appointments on her calendar, Chase watched the expressions flit across her face. Frustration, annoyance and then finally resignation. Removing her hand, she spoke into the phone. "Tenley, I see you have a crazy schedule today, so I'm going to call you back at six o'clock tonight. Please be there."

Chase wondered if she realized she would need to wake up at two-thirty in the morning in order to place the call. He didn't mind getting up at that hour, but he was trained to get by on very little sleep. Kate, on the other hand, had shadows beneath her eyes and he knew the extreme heat was sapping whatever energy she had left. With jet lag already kicking in, he suspected it would take more than an alarm clock to rouse her from a sound sleep at that hour. He found he was looking forward to the task.

She hung up the phone and looked at him. "Well, hopefully she'll listen to her voicemail messages."

"I'm sure she will," he said smoothly. "We'll come back in time to make the call."

She nodded, looking around, her gaze lingering on a plastic container on his desk filled with red and black licorice drops. They were his one weakness.

"May I?" she asked, indicating the candy.

"Sure, help yourself."

He watched as she unscrewed the top and reached in to take just two of the small drops. A stack of his mail lay next to the candy, and he didn't miss how she furtively scanned the top envelope as she replaced the cover on the canister.

"Thanks," she murmured, delicately popping a candy into her mouth. "Is this really where you live?"

"More like where I sleep, at least when I'm here, which isn't often. I don't spend that much time on the base." He frowned, having told her way more than he'd intended. "C'mon, I'll show you where you'll be staying."

He opened the door of his CHU, and after she'd stepped outside, turned back and grabbed the jar of licorice drops and shoved them into his backpack. Chase followed her to the Humvee, glad to be out of the confines of the CHU. As they drove across the base, he wondered how she would react when she saw the accommodations the USO had arranged for her. When they pulled up in front of a cluster of khaki-brown army tents, he sensed her confusion.

"Here we are," he said briskly, getting out of the vehicle and retrieving her duffel bag and his backpack. He waved the driver on, and Kate watched in dismay as the Humvee rumbled out of sight along the dusty road.

"What do you mean, 'here we are'?" she asked, coming to stand beside him.

She stared at the nearest tent, which Chase silently acknowledged looked as if it had seen both world wars. The canvas was faded in spots and sported patches and duct tape where the fabric had ripped or the tent had sprung a leak. The outside had been stacked with sandbags for protection and for insulation, as the temperatures could drop below freezing at night. Several female soldiers came out of the tent, their weapons over their shoulders. They gave Chase and Kate curious looks as they passed. Chase could hear feminine voices from inside.

"This is the best the USO could provide for sleeping quarters," he explained. "I hope you don't mind bunking with the troops for one night."

He watched as Kate pushed back the flap that covered the entry. Two dozen or more army cots were lined on either side of the interior. Several female soldiers were stowing their gear in foot lockers, and the floor was covered with duffel bags and military gear. The women gave Kate a nod, but otherwise ignored both her and Chase. One cot was conspicuously free of gear, with only a pillow and a tightly rolled sleeping bag placed at the foot.

"I'm assuming that's where I'm sleeping?" Kate asked Chase, eyeballing the empty bunk.

"You would assume correctly."

Kate gave him a helpless look that went straight to Chase's protective instincts. He silently cursed Colonel Decker for giving him this assignment, because he was within two seconds of telling her she could bunk with him in his CHU. Or without him in his CHU. He'd pretty much give her whatever she wanted if she would just stop looking at him like that. He reminded himself that he was an Army Ranger, a member of an elite force able to operate in any environment. Unless it was within fifty feet of a woman like Kate Fitzgerald.

Kate put her hands together and drew in a deep breath. "Okay. This is okay. I can definitely sleep here. Can you tell me where my client and her band will sleep when they arrive?"

"The concert will be held over at the parade field. There's an administrative building nearby that the USO will use to house the bands while they're here, but it hasn't been converted yet."

"Would it be possible to see it?"

"Absolutely," he assured her. "Why don't you stow your gear, and then we'll grab something to eat at the dining facility before we head over there? I don't know about you, but I could use a good meal."

Hefting her pink duffel over her shoulder, Kate walked into the tent, and Chase could almost read her thoughts as she stared around her. The walls were reinforced with plywood, and army blankets hung from the roof supports between several of the cots, providing a minimal amount of privacy. As she stepped inside, Kate's footsteps echoed on the plywood floor.

Seeing it through her eyes, Chase had to admit that it looked pretty bleak. Overhead, a large, flexible tube ran the length of the tent and pumped in cool air, but it couldn't compete with the blistering temperatures outside and the interior was stifling hot and smelled like musty canvas.

Dropping her duffel bag onto the empty cot, she turned to him with an overly bright smile. "This will be great," she assured him. "After all, it's not like I'll be doing anything except sleeping, right?"

He had another decadent vision of her, this time straddling his hips as he lay on one of the narrow cots. Oh, yeah. He'd been outside the wire for way too long. He'd told Kate point-blank that he had no intention of sleeping with her.

He'd lied.

4

KATE TRIED NOT TO LET Chase Rawlins see how completely horrified she was by the sleeping quarters he'd secured for her. Clearly, he belonged in this kind of Spartan, militaristic environment. He probably thrived on danger. He certainly looked as if he did.

Casting a dubious eye around the tent, she wondered how many spiders or other multilegged critters waited in the shadows.

Two soldiers lounged on their cots, chatting idly. Neither of them seemed concerned about eight-legged bunkmates, and Kate decided that if they could sleep in this tent, so could she. Pulling her small handbag out of her tote, she determinedly joined her chaperone outside the tent.

"So, can I call you Chase, or is there some kind of military protocol that demands you be addressed by your title?" she asked as they began walking across the base to the dining facility. "I'm sorry. I peeked at the mail on your desk. That *is* your name, isn't it?"

He slanted her an amused look. "It is. I have no objection to you calling me Chase, unless there are uniforms nearby, and then I would prefer you address me as Major Rawlins."

"Well, you can call me Kate even if there are other people around," she said, unable to resist the urge to tease him just a little. He was much too serious. "I prefer it, actually. I feel old when you call me Miss Fitzgerald."

Chase swept her with an all-encompassing look that missed nothing and caused heat to bloom low in her abdomen.

"I find that hard to believe," he finally said, "considering you're like…what, twenty-five?"

"Ha!" Kate gave a bark of laughter. "Thank you, but now I know you're trying to flatter me. I just turned thirty-one."

She could see by his expression that she'd surprised him.

"Really? I didn't think you were much older than your client. Maybe it's the freckles."

Kate couldn't suppress the pleasure she felt at knowing he had thought she was younger than she actually was. Unless he figured she was immature? He'd already implied she was nuts for having come over here by herself, when clearly no other celebrity representatives had felt the need to do so. But what he didn't know was that her relationship with Tenley went beyond business. Tenley was more than just a client, more than just a sister. Tenley was like her own child, and she'd do whatever she needed to do to ensure her comfort and safety.

"I used to hate my freckles for that exact reason," she said ruefully. "People always thought I was younger than I am."

"I don't know," he said, studying her face. "I like them."

To her dismay, Kate felt herself blushing. "That's because you've never had them or been teased about them. Just how old are you?"

He grinned. "I'll turn thirty-one next month."

So they were essentially the same age. Kate felt a wave of relief, which was ridiculous. It wasn't as if she had any interest in Chase Rawlins, regardless of his age. But a little voice whispered that she was a liar.

"When do the dining facilities open in the morning?" Kate asked, in an effort to move the subject to safer ground. She so did not need to be thinking about him in a romantic way. "Please don't tell me I have to be up at some ungodly hour or risk going without breakfast."

"For the most part, the peak hours are during the traditional meal times. But we also have a midnight chow, and then the dining facilities open for the day at 4:00 a.m." He slanted her a quick grin. "Don't worry. I'll make sure you don't go hungry."

Kate felt her pulse leap at his smile, and wondered how he would react if she told him she wasn't hungry for food, but for him. Shocked by her own thoughts, she focused her attention on her surroundings. As they walked between the rows of tents and housing units, Kate's feet kicked up dust and despite the fact the sun was dropping lower on the horizon, the intense heat hadn't yet begun to abate.

"How do you tolerate the climate?" she murmured, passing a hand over her eyes. "I've never felt so hot."

"Believe it or not, you do get used to it. In fact, it gets surprisingly cold at night."

Kate cast an appraising eye toward the mountains, where the sun was just touching the peaks. She'd heard that the desert grew cold at night, but right now she had a hard time believing it. "I'll take your word for it."

Chase stopped in front of a long building constructed of corrugated metal. "These are the female facilities. The men's showers are just on the other side. If you'd like, I'll wait for you here."

Kate stepped inside the women's bathroom, relieved to see there were plenty of shower stalls. Traveling for forty-eight hours had left her feeling sticky and uncomfortable, and she couldn't wait to get back here with a bar of soap and a change of clothes.

She washed her hands and then splashed cool water on her face, studying her reflection in the mirror over the sink. She looked pale. Her freckles stood out starkly against her skin, and her hair was coming loose from the ponytail holder. Pulling it free, she combed her fingers through it and then secured it in a loose knot at the back of her head. Pinching some color into her cheeks, she rejoined Chase outside. Reaching into his pocket, he withdrew a small, plastic device and handed it to her. Kate realized it was a beeper.

"If you need to use the bathroom during the middle of the night," he said carefully, "I want you to ask one of the female soldiers to walk here with you, or I want you to contact me. This is a beeper that goes directly to my phone. Just press this button, and I'll be at your tent in under five minutes. I'll walk here with you."

"I'm sure I can walk to the bathroom by myself," she said, studying the small device. Raising her gaze, she gave him a leering smile in an effort to lighten him up a little. "Unless, of course, you want to scrub my back."

To her astonishment, two ruddy spots appeared high on his cheeks and he stared at her for a moment as if he thought she might actually be serious. Kate waited breathlessly for his response.

"This is a combat environment, Miss Fitzgerald," he finally said, dragging his gaze from hers. "There are more than twenty thousand troops stationed here, and while I can personally vouch for my own men, I can't say with one-hundred-percent certainty that you would be safe walking across the base at night. So I need you to promise me that you'll ask one of the female soldiers to accompany you, or you'll contact me, understood?"

Kate swallowed. There was no way she'd call this guy in the middle of the night for any purpose, especially not one so personal. Just the thought of being alone with him after dark caused her imagination to surge. "I'm sure the last thing you want to do is escort me to the ladies' room."

"My job is to keep you safe. If you decide to go somewhere without me, I can't guarantee that safety. So you *will* call me."

His tone said clearly that it wasn't a request, and Kate nodded as she dropped the beeper into her pocketbook. "Okay," she promised. "I'll call you. But only if you stop calling me Miss Fitzgerald and start calling me Kate. Jeez."

They walked in silence after that, until they reached a large complex of buildings. Dozens of soldiers milled around outside, smoking cigarettes or talking, while other groups walked past them with purposeful steps.

"Here we are," Chase said, pulling open a door to a large building as Kate breathed in the enticing aromas of roast chicken and grilled hamburgers.

The dining facility was essentially an enormous cafeteria, complete with soup and salad bars, a drink fountain, separate lines for hot entrees or sandwiches, and one section for desserts. There must have been at least five hundred soldiers either eating at the long tables, or waiting in line, and the noise level was so cheerful and normal that Kate had a difficult time remembering that they were in Afghanistan. The air-conditioning was a welcome relief from the dry, dusty heat outside, and she wanted to slither to the ground and press her overheated skin against the cool tiles.

"C'mon," Chase said, accurately reading her thoughts. "Let's start you with a salad and plenty of fluids. Traveling can dehydrate you, and I don't need you to become sick."

He steered her toward the salad bar and, without asking her what she preferred, took a plate and began heaping it with salad greens and toppings.

"Is that for me?" she asked doubtfully.

"What?" he demanded. "You don't like salad?" He ran a critical eye over her. "Looks to me like that's all you eat."

Kate grimaced and took the plate from him. "Trust me," she said drily, "I can wipe out an entire container of Cherry Garcia ice cream in one sitting and still not feel satisfied."

To her surprise, he laughed. "I'd like to see that."

She stared at him, transfixed by the way his smile changed his face. His teeth gleamed white in the sunburned bronze of his skin, and she felt a nearly irresistible urge to press her fingertips into the deep indents of his dimples. His grin was so captivating that Kate had a ridiculous sense of pleasure that she had been the one to cause it.

"Well, maybe one day you will," she found herself saying as she returned his smile. In the next instant, she realized he would never see her gorge herself on ice cream. She would only be in his company for the next few days, until Tenley arrived, and then she would likely have no more opportunity—or reason—to share meals with him. Or anything else, for that matter. She found the thought oddly depressing.

"When you've finished building your salad," Chase said, "grab a seat at one of the tables over there. I'll go get us something a little more substantial to eat. What do you like… chicken, beef, pasta?"

Turning, Kate studied the menu board at the front of the food line. "I'll try some of the fried chicken. And mashed potatoes."

Chase nodded. "Good choice. It's kinda hard to screw up chicken and potatoes."

Kate watched as he turned and walked away, telling herself that she was *not* admiring his ass. But it was an effort to drag her attention back to putting toppings on her salad. She was vaguely aware of the interested glances she drew from several nearby soldiers, dressed as she was in a turquoise blouse and white jeans. Finally, she pulled a bottle

of water from a cooler and selected a seat in the far corner
of the cafeteria, where it was less crowded.

She picked at her salad, keeping one eye on Chase as he
moved through the line, piling a tray with plates of food.
When he finally made his way through the cafeteria toward
her, she noticed how several female soldiers turned to watch
his progress. She couldn't blame them. Major Chase Rawlins had a combination of good looks and an easy confidence
that captured your attention and then held it.

He placed the tray on the table and began unloading the
plates. Kate stared in astonishment at the heaping servings
of fried chicken and mashed potatoes that he had chosen for
her. But that couldn't compare with the double helpings of
two different entrees that he had taken for himself. And he
had no less than three bottles of chilled water.

"Are you going to eat all that?" she asked, before she
could prevent herself.

But instead of looking insulted, he merely grinned. "Oh,
yeah. I've been surviving on MREs for the past two weeks.
This is going to be sheer ambrosia."

"MREs?" she asked, taking a mouthful of potatoes.
"What is that?"

"Meals Ready to Eat, although some of the troops like
to call them Meals Rejected by Everybody, or Meals Rarely
Edible. They're prepackaged meals in a pouch, designed to
provide the soldier with all the basic caloric and nutritional
requirements for one day. They're basically field rations."

"Not so appetizing?"

Chase shrugged as he dug into a plate heaped with baked
ziti. "They do the job. I don't pay much attention to what I
eat when I'm in the field."

Kate could well believe that. He struck her as the kind of
man capable of intense focus. If he was on a mission, one
hundred percent of his attention would be on his work, not

on food. She could easily envision him skipping meals simply because he was too busy to eat. But right now, he made short work of his dinner, devouring it with gusto.

"So what is it that you do, exactly?" she asked.

He glanced up, and quickly wiped his mouth with a napkin. "The usual."

Kate gave him a half smile. "Which is…what, exactly? You said you've been in the field for the past two weeks. What do you do when you're 'in the field'?"

Chase shrugged and took a long swallow of water, nearly draining the bottle. "A lot of nothing, actually." He gave her a quick smile. "At least, nothing very exciting."

He wasn't going to give her any information, she realized, studying his bland expression.

"Is it normal for soldiers to grow beards? I thought there was some strict protocol about being clean-shaven."

He smoothed his hand over his jaw, and Kate found herself wondering how his beard would feel against her skin. Would it be soft or bristly? If he nuzzled her neck, would he leave a rash? Disconcerted by the direction of her thoughts, she fixed her attention on her food, pushing it around the plate.

"Well, there wasn't much opportunity for a close shave while I was out there," he said offhandedly. "I got back to base just before you arrived, so not much chance to clean up, either. Sorry."

"So how did you end up becoming my escort?" she asked, her curiosity getting the better of her. "I don't know much about the military, but if I had to guess I'd say you were special forces. They're the only ones who get to grow facial hair, right? So why would they assign someone like you to bring me to the different concert sites? I promise you I'm not dangerous."

Chase stopped eating the second she suggested he was

special forces, and listened to her with a combination of amusement and surprise. But when she said she wasn't dangerous, he gave a soft laugh and muttered something under his breath that sounded suspiciously like, "you have no idea."

Now he sat back in his chair and considered her. "Okay," he said, a smile still tilting his lips. "You're right. I'm an Army Ranger, part of a special-operations unit. But my team screwed up on a recent operation and so here I am—" he gestured expansively with his hands "—anxious to prove to my commanding officer that I can complete this assignment without incident."

"Ah," she said, meaningfully. "So this is sort of like a punishment for you." Leaning forward, she lowered her voice to a conspiratorial whisper. "I promise to be on my best behavior."

"Uh-huh." His voice said he didn't believe her, but he couldn't hide the dimples that dented his cheeks, evidence of his amusement. "If I can't handle one woman, then I have no business being an Army Ranger."

Kate laughed in astonishment. "Oh, wow. Be careful what you say. That just sounded like a challenge."

Chase grinned. "Going to give me a run for my money?"

"I just might." Kate let her gaze drift over him. She watched his hands as he toyed with the saltshaker. They were a lot like him, lean and strong. She wondered how they would feel on her body. "I'd be doing you a favor. After all, I wouldn't want you to get soft, considering your current assignment is so easy."

He snapped his eyes to hers. "Trust me," he said drily. "There's no chance of that happening around you." Before she could register what he'd said, he stood up. "Are you going to finish your meal?"

Kate pushed the plate away. "No, I don't think so. I'm

actually not that hungry. What I'd really like is to head over to where the first concert event will be held."

Chase nodded and began stacking their plates on his tray. "No problem."

She watched as he disposed of their dishes, her heart still thumping unevenly. Had he meant his words the way she had interpreted them? That she aroused him physically? The very thought sent hot blood surging through her veins. She wondered what had happened to get him pulled off his last assignment. He had made light of it, but Kate could see it bothered him. She didn't know him at all, but guessed he would much rather be back in the field with his men than here with her. Especially if he found himself attracted to her. She didn't know him well, but guessed that he was the kind of guy who would keep his professional and private lives completely separate. And right now, she was definitely part of his professional life.

When he returned to the table, she drew in a deep breath. "Listen, Chase, if you'd rather not take me over to the concert site, I'm sure I can get someone else to go with me. I understand that this probably isn't your favorite thing to do."

"No chance," he said smoothly. "You've been assigned to me, and I'll be the only one to take you over there."

She'd been assigned to him. As if she were nothing more than a number, or an unpleasant project that he just needed to get done. Realistically, she knew that wasn't true, but in that instant she realized she wanted him to see her as more than a task or an assignment. She wanted him to see her as a woman.

"Okay." She stood up and pushed her chair in. "Then let's do this."

Outside, the sun had finally dipped behind the mountains and the base was quickly growing dark. Kate welcomed the change, both because the temperature had dropped and because the indistinct light made it more difficult for Major Rawlins to read her expression. They walked in silence, and she didn't miss how he adjusted his stride so that she could keep up with him. She was fading quickly from sheer exhaustion. Part of her wanted to suggest that they wait until morning to view the concert site, but the stubborn part of her—the part that wanted to impress this tough man—refused to capitulate.

Thankfully, the parade field wasn't far from the dining facility. A large stage had been constructed at one end of the field, and an enormous American flag had been hung behind it as a patriotic backdrop. Dozens of heavy-duty extension cords snaked across the ground near the stage, and two tall light poles provided illumination.

"This is where the bands will perform," Chase said, kicking several of the cords out of her way. "Of course, it will look much different once all the equipment is set up."

Kate walked around the stage, silently acknowledging that it would more than suffice for Tenley's band. She had brought her planner with her, and she jotted down notes as they surveyed the site.

"How far back will the audience be from the performers?" She measured off several paces from the front of the stage. "I don't want them too close, and I'm going to insist on security personnel to keep the crowds back."

Chase laughed softly and scratched the bridge of his nose. "I don't know what kind of audiences your client performs for, but this isn't a Texas roadhouse. This is the U.S. military, and they will be respectful."

Kate frowned, wanting to believe him, but recalling at least one instance when Tenley had been accosted by a fan who had breached the security and climbed onto the stage.

"Look at me," Chase said, and put his hands on her shoulders, dipping his head to stare directly into her eyes. "I will keep Tenley Miles safe, okay? You can trust me."

Kate searched his eyes and realized that she did trust him. He was bigger than life, a guy who obviously took his job seriously. Knowing that she could rely on him was an amazing feeling. She'd always had to be the strong one; the person who made all the decisions and ensured everything went smoothly. That this man was willing to take that burden from her meant more to her than she could express.

"Thank you," she said. "Tenley has already had one bad experience with a fan."

"You have my word that nothing like that will happen here," he said firmly. "But I'll arrange to have military police positioned around the stage and throughout the audience."

"Thank you. May I see the administrative building where the performers will stay?"

Chase preceded her through the large building directly behind the stage. Immediately inside the doors was a spacious auditorium where the band members could relax while waiting to perform.

"I'm not familiar with the exact details," Chase said as they walked through the room, "but I understand the USO will set up food and drink stations for the performers, and they'll have access to pretty much whatever they need."

The space was more than generous, and Kate could easily envision Tenley relaxing here as she prepared to perform. Even with other entertainers using the room, there was little likelihood that Tenley would feel crowded. Kate nodded her approval and took some more notes. Once she left here, it would be easy to get the sites confused, and she wanted to go over everything in advance with Tenley, so that her sister would know what to expect.

Leaving the auditorium, Chase led her down a main corridor and showed her several rooms that were in the process of being converted to bunk rooms for the entertainers. Try as she might, Kate couldn't find anything to criticize. Granted, the accommodations weren't luxurious, but they were adequate for Tenley's needs, especially considering they were on a military base in Afghanistan.

After snapping the lights off in the last room and closing the door, Kate fell into step beside Chase as they made their way back through the building to the parade field.

"Well, it certainly appears that the USO has thought of everything," Kate remarked as they stepped outside. "Will I have an opportunity to meet with the USO coordinators tomorrow? Tenley has some, um, unique requirements that I'd like to address with them."

Chase cast her one swift, questioning look. "Like what?"

"Well, she's deathly afraid of buses, so I want to be sure that she won't have to travel in one, not even from the flight line to where she'll be staying."

"Okay," he said quietly. "Can I ask why?"

"Her parents were killed in a bus crash when she was just six years old. Tenley was trapped in the wreckage with them for several hours before rescue crews could free her."

"Jesus," he breathed. "Poor kid."

Kate gave him a grateful look. "She claims not to remember anything about the crash, but some nights she has terrible nightmares."

Chase nodded. "The USO would normally transport all the entertainers in a troop bus, but I can arrange for a private vehicle to pick her up at the terminal. Anything else?"

"Just that I need to stay with her, in her sleeping quarters."

"Because of the nightmares?"

Kate nodded. "Something like that."

"Shouldn't be a problem."

Kate glanced at him, surprised at how easily he accepted Tenley's needs and agreed to accommodate them. In an-

other place and time, Chase Rawlins was exactly the kind
of man that she would have given anything to be with, even
for just one night.

They walked in silence toward the tent where Kate would
sleep, but she could almost hear the gears turning in his
head.

"You've been great," she finally said, breaking the silence. "About everything. And I can't tell you how much
it means to me. I had a lot of anxiety, not knowing what to
expect, but so far you've managed to alleviate all my fears."

They reached her tent and he turned to face her. "I hope
so," he said quietly. "I don't want you to be afraid of anything while you're here. That's why you have me."

His words caused her imagination to surge, and suddenly
she wanted to know what it would be like to have him—to
really have him. For one night, or for as many nights as she
might be here. But she also knew she lacked the courage required to make any kind of move on him. He didn't wear a
wedding band, but that didn't mean he wasn't already committed to someone else. So she just nodded, acknowledging
the small promise he *was* able to give her.

"I do have a question, though," he said, watching her
closely. "I'm pretty good at reading people, and there's something I just can't figure out."

"What's that?"

"I don't know anything about Tenley Miles, but I do know
that your devotion to her seems to go beyond that of other
entertainers and their publicists." He paused. "Am I wrong?"

Few people knew that Kate and Tenley were even related,
never mind sisters. They didn't share the same last name,
nor did they look at all alike, so no one made the connec-
tion and it wasn't something they publicized. Kate had no
problem with anyone knowing about their relationship, but
much of Tenley's popularity stemmed from the fact that she

was the orphaned child of two famous entertainers. The fact
that she'd been left alone in the world yet still managed to
overcome her personal tragedy to fulfill her musical des-
tiny was like a fairytale. If people knew that she'd actually
had an adult sister who had dropped everything in order to
be at her side and raise her, that fairytale would lose some
of its luster. So when Tenley had first shown signs of being
musically gifted, Kate had decided to present herself as Tenley's publicist, rather than her sister.

"No," she said, looking at Chase. "You're not wrong. Tenley is my sister. Well, my half sister, actually. If I'm a little
overprotective, it's because she's been through so much."

His face registered his surprise, but he quickly schooled
his features. "That makes sense. So did you also lose a parent in that bus crash?"

Kate nodded. "My mother. But I was eighteen at that
point, and accustomed to being on my own. Her death hit
Tenley a lot harder."

Chase looked at her for a long moment, and Kate wondered what he was thinking. Finally, he stepped back.

"Well, she's lucky to have you," he said. "You look beat,
so I'm going to let you turn in."

"Okay," she said, nodding. "Thanks again. For everything." Kate turned toward the tent and then looked back at
him. "So I'll see you in the morning?"

"If not sooner," he said, and closed one eye in a conspiratorial wink.

Kate knew her mouth opened, but before she could ask
what he meant, he turned and walked away. Slowly, she entered the tent and got ready for bed. His words echoed in
her head, and she knew she'd never sleep.

5

KATE WAS AWAKENED BY someone shaking her shoulder. She tried to bury herself deeper in her covers, but there was no escaping.

"Time to wake up, Kate."

The masculine voice shocked her into action and she sat up, heart pounding. Disoriented, Kate blinked at the hard-eyed soldier who stood over her, holding a flashlight directed at the ground. The indirect light was sufficient for her to make out Chase Rawlins's features. For a moment, she had no idea where she was, or why she was sleeping in a tent. Then everything came rushing back, and her gaze snapped to the entrance.

"What time is it?"

"Oh-dot-dark." His low voice was laced with amusement.

Kate could see it was still pitch black outside. "Why are you here?"

"Didn't you promise to call your sister?"

Kate stared up at Chase, bewildered. Looking around her, she could just make out the shapeless lumps of the other women asleep on their cots. "Yes," she whispered fiercely. "At six o'clock, not the middle of the night."

"I'm sorry to tell you that on the East Coast of the United

States, it's almost six o'clock in the evening. They're eight and a half hours behind us. If you still want to make that call, you'd better hustle."

With a groan, Kate realized she hadn't considered the extreme time difference. She was half tempted to change her mind about calling Tenley, but in her mind's eye she saw her sister waiting to hear from her. If she didn't place the call, Tenley would be frantic. She'd think the worst and put herself through hell. Kate couldn't do that to her.

She scrubbed her hands over her face. "Okay, fine. Give me ten minutes."

"You've got five. I'll wait for you outside."

She watched the bobbing light of his flashlight as he crossed the tent and disappeared through the flap, and decided she would need to speak to someone about tightening up the security on the sleeping quarters.

Pushing back the sleeping bag, she swung her legs to the floor, shivering in the predawn chill. Her eyes felt gritty and every muscle in her body ached with exhaustion. Fumbling on the floor beneath her cot, she found her shoes and pulled them on, not bothering to change into street clothes. Her flannel lounge pants and long-sleeve top were adequate, and would enable her to jump right back into bed after she'd talked with Tenley.

Despite her exhaustion, she'd been right about not being able to fall asleep after Chase had left her. Her biggest surprise had come when she'd unzipped her duffel bag and discovered a jar of licorice inside. It was the same jar from Chase's housing unit, and she realized he must have stashed it in her bag after she'd made that first failed telephone call to Tenley. She found the gesture oddly touching.

She'd lain awake thinking about him. Now she understood what he'd meant when he'd said he would see her sooner than the morning, but at the time her imagination had conjured up all kinds of erotic fantasies about him. On top of that, the cot was uncomfortable, and she was unaccustomed to sleeping in such close quarters with other people. The unfamiliar sounds of the base had kept her awake until finally she'd fallen into a fitful sleep, only to be wakened by Chase.

Yawning hugely, she pulled back the flap of the tent and found Chase standing just outside. His eyes swept over her, taking in every detail of her lounge pants and thin top, lingering just a little too long on her breasts. Glancing down, Kate saw her nipples were stiff from the cold and poked against the fabric of her shirt. She crossed her arms over her chest.

"You realize that I only fell asleep like fifteen minutes ago," she said crossly. "Why didn't you tell me I'd need to wake up at two-thirty in the morning if I wanted to talk to Tenley? I could have chosen a different time."

"Do you want to make the call or not?"

Kate frowned at his impatient tone, and guessed that he was no happier about being awake at this hour than she was. Her bones ached and she actually felt a little sick. More than anything, she wanted to crawl back into her cot and sleep, but she'd told Tenley she would call her, and she intended to make good on her word.

"Yes."

"Then let's go."

Without waiting for her response, he turned and walked away while Kate watched in dismay. He gave a low whistle and a dark shape materialized from the shadows. A dog trotted toward him, its tail wagging enthusiastically as Chase reached down and gave it a friendly rub behind the ears. The animal wore a harness and stayed close to Chase's side.

The night air was chilly, and for a brief second Kate debated on going back for a sweater, but Chase wasn't waiting for her. With a sound of frustration, she followed him. The roads were covered with small rocks, which made walking treacherous when you couldn't see where you were going. After she'd stumbled twice, Chase finally stopped and waited for her to catch up, using his flashlight to illuminate her path.

"So, did you wake up just so I could make my phone call, or do you not sleep?" Kate asked, hugging herself around the middle and trying to keep her teeth from chattering. She wouldn't have been at all surprised if Chase responded that he didn't require sleep; he was a machine.

"I caught some sleep, but I don't need much to get by."

"Will you go back to bed after this?" she asked, partly because she was interested, and partly because she was just trying to make conversation.

"Well, I guess that depends," he mused.

Kate shot him a startled look. Had she only imagined the sexual suggestion in his voice? She tried to read his expression, but the darkness made it nearly impossible.

"Actually," he continued smoothly, "I'm up for the day."

Kate should have felt relieved, but found his words left her oddly deflated. She remembered what he had said earlier that day: *I have no intention of sleeping with you.* Either the change in time zones had seriously messed with her biorhythms, or she had definitely gone too long without sex, because she spent way too much time imagining him naked. "Who's your friend?" she asked, in an effort to change the subject. Kate tried to pat the dog, but the animal shied away from her hand.

"This is Charity."

"Ah," she said meaningfully.

Chase looked at her. "What does that mean?"

Kate shrugged. "When you and the other guys were talking about Charity, I thought you had a girlfriend on the base. I never would have guessed you were talking about a dog."

"Well, I think Charity would disagree. I'm pretty sure she thinks she's human."

"So, do you?"

"What?"

"Have a girlfriend?"

He gave a surprised laugh. "No, I do not. Right now, Charity is the only female in my life." He glanced at her. "Aside from you, of course."

Kate had already noticed that he wore no rings, but felt a surge of satisfaction in knowing he was single.

"Where did you get her?" she asked, moving to safer territory.

"She was a stray that I rescued from a village in the mountains. I guess you could say we adopted each other."

"Do you keep her in your housing unit?"

"She won't come inside, but when I'm on base she'll sleep outside my door. When I'm in the field, I leave her with the K-9 unit. She gets along with the other dogs, and the handlers have been teaching her how to track."

The mention of his housing unit reminded her of the small gift he had left in her duffel bag. "By the way, thank you for the licorice. I feel guilty that you gave it to me."

"Don't." He rubbed a hand over his flat stomach. "I try to avoid sweets, but I can't resist licorice drops. It's better if you take them. Besides, my mother will send another jar in her next care package."

They had reached his housing unit, and Kate welcomed the warmth of the interior after the chill of the night air. As Chase dialed an outside line, she stood in the middle of the room and looked around. Although she had already been inside his unit once, everything looked different at night.

A desk lamp cast a warm glow, making the room seem almost cozy.

While Chase was concentrating on the phone, she took a covert peek into his bedroom. Disappointingly, his bed was neatly made and there was nothing to indicate that he had slept there at all. She would have enjoyed seeing rumpled blankets or clothes on the floor—anything to indicate the guy wasn't completely perfect.

"Something interesting in there?" Chase asked, catching her.

Kate flushed. "I was, uh, just checking out your bed."

His eyes grew hot, and Kate's body responded instantly. Her breathing quickened and her imagination surged with images of the two of them, naked and entwined in his sheets. She would have sworn those same images were swirling through his head, too, but then he thrust the phone receiver at her, breaking whatever spell she had been under.

"Make your call," he growled, and spun away.

Keeping a wary eye on him, Kate quickly dialed Tenley's number, frustrated when the call went to voicemail.

"Tenley, it's Katie. I told you that I'd be calling. Why aren't you there?" She lowered her voice. "I don't want you to worry about anything, okay? Russell will drive you to the airport tonight, and I'll be right here waiting for you when you arrive. Okay, I'll try to call you later."

She hung up the phone and stood for a moment, chewing the edge of her finger. Where was Tenley and why wasn't she answering the phone? She briefly considered calling Russell to ask him to check on her sister, and just as quickly discarded the idea. She'd asked both the housekeeper and Russell to keep an eye on Tenley and she trusted they would. There was a reasonable explanation for why her sister wasn't answering the phone. She was not going to freak out, especially not when there wasn't anything she could do about it.

She blew out a hard breath. "She's not home."

"Jeez, what a surprise," Chase said drily. Seeing Kate's annoyed expression, he spread his hands. "What? She's not exactly Miss Responsible. If she was, you wouldn't be here."

"What is that supposed to mean?"

Chase gave her a tolerant look. "C'mon, Kate, don't play coy with me. We both know that the only reason you're here is to try and save your sister's career."

Kate desperately wanted to tell him he was wrong and that Tenley was coming over for all the right reasons. But seeing the truth in Chase's eyes took the fight out of her. Plunking herself down on the nearby chair, she dropped her head into her hands.

"You're right," she admitted in a weary voice. "I'm not even sure she'll come. I should have stayed behind and flown here with her, but she actually seemed excited about the prospect of coming." Raising her head, she looked helplessly at Chase. "What if she doesn't get on that plane? I mean, I can't make her. I just thought if I came first and assured her that it wasn't nearly as scary as everyone made her believe, then she wouldn't be so reluctant."

To her surprise, Chase dropped to his haunches in front of her, putting him at eye-level with her. He placed a hand on either side of her seat, effectively trapping her.

"I think what you're doing is completely harebrained," he said, but his sympathetic smile took most of the sting out of his words. "But I also think Tenley Miles is very lucky to have you on her side. I don't see any other publicists over here doing this for their clients."

Kate gave him a rueful smile. "That's just because they're not related."

"The bottom line is, if she isn't willing to do what it takes to fix the mess she made, then that's her problem, not yours.

At some point, Kate, you need to let her take responsibility for her own life."

Kate stared at him, knowing he was right. "That sounds easy in theory, but you don't know Tenley. She's just a kid. She couldn't find her own way across the street without someone to help her. The music industry would eat her alive. She *needs* me."

Chase pushed to his feet and stood looking down at her, and Kate could almost read his mind. He thought she was nuts.

"Look," she reasoned, "maybe I am a little overprotective, but trust me when I say you would feel the same way if you met her. She brings out the protective instinct in everyone." Kate gave a soft laugh. "Even you wouldn't be immune."

"It is hard for me to imagine that someone who's been in the public spotlight since she was young could have any vulnerability left," Chase said wryly.

Kate looked down at her hands. "Maybe that's what makes her so vulnerable."

"You were pretty young when your mother died," he said quietly. "It couldn't have been easy for you, either. What I don't get is why I didn't know that the famous country singer, Willa Dean, had another daughter. Hell, I'm not sure anybody knows."

Kate shrugged. "My mother was still in high school when she became pregnant with me. She and my dad tried to make a go of it, but she had her heart set on becoming a super-star, and he just wanted to be a car mechanic. They were only kids."

"So what happened?"

"They split up before I was a year old. I traveled with my mother and her band for the first six years of my life, until I started elementary school. Then I went to live with my dad and his new wife."

"That's rough," Chase said. "Were you happy with your father?"

Kate sighed, remembering. "I wasn't unhappy. But he and his wife had a new baby and hardly any money. Things were tough for a couple of years and I always had the sense that I was a burden. But then my mother started selling albums and she began to send some money to my father for my upkeep. That helped."

"Did you ever go back and live with her?"

Kate didn't look at him. "No," she said quietly. "My mother rose to the top of the billboard charts very quickly, and she didn't have time for a kid." She gave a rueful laugh. "Even after she had Tenley, she didn't have time for a kid. Sometimes, I think the only reason she brought Tenley on tour with her was because it helped her public image. She dragged that poor baby everywhere, and what the public didn't see was that when the cameras weren't around, Tenley rarely saw her mother. She spent most of her time with a nanny. But when people thought of Willa Dean, they automatically thought of her angelic little daughter. So when she died..." Her voice trailed off.

"You became Tenley's mother."

Kate laughed, refusing to dwell on those days. "Well, more like a doting aunt." She slanted him an amused look. "Were you a Willa Dean fan?"

Chase chuckled. "Still am. I'm from Texas, and there's nothing a Texas boy loves more than a good old country song. Man, I grew up listening to Willa Dean, and it didn't hurt that she was so damned gorgeous. In fact, my brother had a poster of her hung over his desk all through high school."

Kate couldn't suppress her smile, not at all surprised to hear that Chase's brother had kept a poster of her mother in his bedroom. She'd been a beautiful woman, and an amazing singer. Everyone had loved Willa Dean, the same way that they now loved her daughter, Tenley.

"Yes, my mother was an incredible woman," she agreed. She yawned hugely. "Oh, my God, I've never been so tired in my life."

Chase pulled her up, his hands strong and warm under her elbows. "C'mon, let's get you into bed. You're asleep on your feet."

"I'll be fine," she assured him. She thought of the long, chilly walk back to the tent and couldn't suppress the shiver that ran through her. "Maybe you have a coat or sweater that I could borrow?"

"I have something even better," he murmured, and turned her toward the rear of the small housing unit. She went, unresisting, until she realized they were in his bedroom. He bent down to pull back the blankets of the bed.

"What are you doing?" Her heart began an unsteady rhythm in her chest as she watched him peel back the sheets. "I'm not sure—"

"Shh," he said soothingly. "Your virtue is safe with me. Lie down and get some sleep."

He pushed her, unresisting, into a sitting position on the edge of the bed, and then crouched down to pull off her shoes. Kate studied his bent head and barely resisted the urge to run her fingers over his velvety short hair.

"Why are you doing this?" she asked. "Aren't there some kind of rules against having members of the opposite sex in your quarters?"

Setting her shoes aside, he looked at her. In the dim light of the bedroom, his eyes seemed to glow in his face. "Yeah," he acknowledged. "There are. But I'm not going to be here. I'm going to head over to command headquarters and catch up on some stuff."

"When will you be back?"

He glanced at his watch. "We'll leave for Camp Leatherneck at 0700 hours, but I'll wake you up well before that."

The temptation he offered was too great to resist. "Okay," she acquiesced. "You win. But I really, really want a hot shower, so if we could work that into the morning routine, I'd appreciate it."

He gave her a brief smile, but there was a tension in his expression that set her pulse tripping. He made a movement to stand up, and Kate impulsively caught his hand in hers. His skin was warm and dry, and she could feel the rough calluses of his palm. He glanced in surprise at their joined hands, and then looked at her face, and for an instant, Kate saw hunger in his eyes.

"Thank you," she murmured, and she leaned forward to press a kiss against his cheek. She meant for the gesture to be quick and impersonal, but he turned his face at the last instant, and her kiss landed on his lips. For a microsecond they both froze, and then Chase made a small sound of defeat and his mouth began moving against hers.

Kate stopped breathing. The guy knew how to kiss. His lips were warm and firm and she found herself tentatively responding. His beard was rough against her sensitive skin, but she didn't care. He didn't touch her except for where his mouth was fused to hers. Kate pressed closer, wanting more of the sensual contact. Chase complied, leisurely slanting his mouth across hers until her lips parted, and he tasted her. The slick contact of his tongue against hers caused heat to explode beneath her skin, and she felt a rush of liquid warmth to her center.

She shifted restlessly, curling her hands around Chase's neck to pull him closer. He made a small groaning sound, and for an instant, Kate thought he would resist. Then he pushed her back against the mattress and covered her body with his.

The sheets were cool through the thin material of her shirt, but Chase's body was warm and Kate dragged him closer, sliding her arms over the sleek muscles of his back. He deepened the kiss, exploring her mouth with his tongue and catching her small moans of pleasure. Kate speared her fingers through the velvet roughness of his short hair, reveling in the feel of it beneath her fingertips.

How long had it been since she'd felt a man's arms around her, or luxuriated in the hardness of a masculine body pressed against her own? Too long, apparently, because she was igniting beneath his touch. She no longer felt tired; every cell in her had come alive. Desire coiled tightly in her womb and then unfurled to radiate through her limbs and finally center at her core, where she pulsed hotly. She wanted to rub herself against him and relieve the ache that was building with every sensuous sweep of his tongue against hers.

Chase dragged his mouth away and Kate had a moment of panic when she thought he was leaving. But he moved his lips to her jaw and pressed hot kisses against her skin until he reached her ear, and then lightly licked along its contours. Kate shuddered and arched her neck to give him better access. He complied, following the path of her throat until he reached the neckline of her shirt. He glanced at her face, and Kate's breath caught at the heat she saw in his eyes.

She didn't object when he slid a hand over one breast and cupped it in his palm. But she was unprepared when he moved his fingers to the hem of her shirt and dragged it upward, exposing her to his hot gaze.

"Christ, you're pretty," he rasped, and slid a callused hand over the smooth skin of her stomach, until he covered one breast.

Kate made a small mewling sound of need and arched upward, wanting more of the sensuous contact. He complied, rubbing his thumb over her nipple and watching as it contracted. Then, as if entranced, he bent his head and kissed the underside of one breast, before drawing her nipple into his mouth, sucking gently on it and laving it with his tongue. She felt an answering tug of need between her legs and instinctively spread her thighs to cradle Chase's hips against her own.

He made an incoherent sound of approval and covered her other breast with his hand as he continued to suckle her. Kate couldn't get enough of him. Boldly, she slid her hands down the length of his back and over the firm rise of his buttocks, pressing him to where she ached for fulfillment. Nothing mattered except the man whose delicious weight pinned her to the mattress.

"You feel so good," she whispered against the top of his head. "I want to feel you inside me."

He groaned loudly, and his mouth stilled. He raised his head and then, almost regretfully, pulled her shirt down, covering her breasts.

Kate frowned, grasping for his hands as she tried to stop him. "What? Why are you stopping? Please don't stop."

But Chase carefully disentangled himself from her limbs and sat up, scrubbing his hands over his face. His breathing sounded uneven, and Kate cautiously sat up, feeling chilled without his warmth.

"That was a mistake," he said in a low voice, not looking at her. "I'm sorry."

"Please don't apologize," she murmured. "This was my fault, not yours."

He angled his head to look at her, and she could see remnants of the earlier heat lingering in his eyes. "My job is to keep you safe, not to take advantage of you."

Kate gave him a wry look. "I'm thirty-one years old, not sixteen. I know what I want."

"Do you? Because I think if you thought this through, you'd realize the last thing you want is a short-lived fling with a guy you'll never see again after this trip."

The thought of never seeing Chase Rawlins again caused a tightening sensation in her chest. She knew he was right, but at that moment, the only thing she wanted was to finish what they had begun and to hell with the consequences. Her job as Tenley's publicist kept her too busy to see anyone seriously, but Chase's touch had reminded her just how much she missed having intimacy in her life, even superficial intimacy with a near stranger. She was pathetic.

Gathering her dignity, she laid a hand on his arm and gave him a forced smile. "You're right. I'm sorry to put you in such an awkward position. I didn't mean to make this any more unpleasant for you than it already is."

"Jesus." Chase gave a disbelieving laugh. "You think that was *unpleasant* for me?" His eyes grew hot. "Do you know how badly I want you?"

Abruptly he stood up, adjusting himself quickly, but not before Kate saw the evidence of his arousal. Her hand fell away from his sleeve, and she pressed her fingers against her mouth, still feeling him there. He stood looking down at her for a long moment, before he dragged a hand over his hair, frustrated.

"I've gotta get out of here." His voice was no more than a husky rasp. "Get some sleep, Kate."

She watched as he left the bedroom, and then she heard the door open and close, followed by the click of a key in the lock. It was the first time he had called her Kate, and she wished she didn't like how it sounded coming from his lips. She lay down and dragged the blankets over her shoulder, staring into the darkness as she replayed the encounter over and over in her mind.

Turning on her side, she bunched the pillow beneath her

cheek. His scent clung to the fabric and she found herself turning her face into the cloth and breathing deeply. Only then did she drift into sleep.

6

"How long will it take us to reach Camp Leatherneck?" Kate asked the following morning, as she rode in the passenger seat of a Humvee, watching Chase drive.

"A couple of hours," he said shortly.

As if by tacit agreement, neither had mentioned the incident from the previous night. But Kate couldn't help but notice that Chase seemed a little short on patience and temper, and she wondered if he regretted what had happened. She hoped he would lighten up a bit, because she wasn't sure she could spend an entire day with him if he was going to be surly.

She studied him furtively as he drove. He wore a clean uniform and a camouflage-patterned baseball cap that was frayed along the brim. He hadn't shaved his beard and he still looked as if he kicked ass for a living. Charity lay obediently on the back seat, and Kate had been surprised to learn the dog would travel with them to each base.

Chase had woken her up before seven o'clock by pounding with his fist on the door of his housing unit until she opened it, bleary-eyed but feeling rested. He, on the other hand, had looked tired and irritable. He'd retrieved her duffel bag and belongings from the women's tent and had given her just ten minutes to dress and meet him outside.

Now they drove across the base, past the housing units and the dining facility. The smell of bacon wafted from the kitchens and her stomach growled loudly, reminding her that she hadn't yet had breakfast.

"Will we have a chance to grab a bite to eat before we leave?" she asked hopefully. "I could really use a cup of coffee."

"Later," he said brusquely. "I have some grub in my bag and we can eat on the way to Camp Leatherneck. But our flight departs in ten minutes and if we're not on board, it leaves without us."

Kate was silent after that. They continued to drive past the parade field, until the only buildings in sight were enormous hangars and storage facilities. But it wasn't until Kate caught sight of a helicopter landing pad, complete with military attack helicopters, that she began to understand just how they would travel to Camp Leatherneck.

"You're kidding," she breathed, and looked over at Chase for confirmation that he was, indeed, just pulling her leg. But he kept his attention fixed on the road, and the only indication that he'd heard her was a small smile that played at the edges of his mouth. "We're flying in a helicopter?"

"Not just a helicopter. A Black Hawk."

He drew the Humvee to a stop at the edge of the helo pad and climbed out of the vehicle, while Kate sat in the passenger seat and peered through the window at the helicopter. Were those rockets strapped to the underside of the small stub wings? Her heart began to thud hard in her chest.

Chase opened the door and waited for her to climb out before he reached in and grabbed their duffel bags and a rucksack. Charity hopped down, her tail wagging in anticipation of this new adventure.

"I brought you something," Chase said, opening the rear of the vehicle.

"A thermos of coffee?" she asked hopefully.

To her surprise, he pulled out a combat helmet and a flak vest. "Try these on for size."

Kate took the helmet from him and put it on, then waited while he fastened it beneath her chin. His fingers brushed the skin of her neck and she tried not to stare at his mouth. He was so close that she could see the tiny scar that bisected his upper lip. She wanted to rub her fingertip over it. When she raised her gaze to his, she found his light green eyes were fastened on her mouth. She had to resist the urge to nervously moisten her lips.

He helped her into the body armor, lifting her arms to tighten the Velcro fastenings on either side. The weight of the metal plates inside the vest were enough to make Kate's shoulders sag.

"Is this really necessary?" she asked, noticing that he wore neither a helmet nor a vest. "We're in a helicopter, after all."

Even without body armor, his uniform, combined with his expression, gave him a distinctly dangerous appearance. He nodded toward her vest. "Those metal plates are the only thing standing between you and a bullet. If we come under attack en route to Camp Leatherneck, you're going to be glad you're wearing them."

Kate knew her face went a little pale. "Is that a possibility?"

"That's always a possibility, Miss Fitzgerald."

"Where is your equipment?" He didn't respond, and Kate suddenly knew why. "Wait. Am I wearing your helmet and flak vest?" She couldn't keep the astonishment out of her voice. "Is that why you're not wearing anything?"

"Don't worry about me." Hefting his rucksack over one

shoulder, he lifted their duffel bags as if they weighed nothing, and handed her shoulder bag to her. "Are you ready?"

She wasn't, but she nodded mutely and followed him and the dog across the tarmac to the waiting helicopter. She felt humbled by the knowledge that he'd given her his protective gear, and his speech about the possibility of coming under attack had dampened her mood.

The sliding door on the side of the aircraft was open, and he threw their gear inside before climbing in. He snapped his fingers and Charity jumped nimbly in, enthusiastically sniffing at the interior before he gave her a command to lie down. Turning, he extended a hand to Kate and helped her up and into the main cabin. There were five soldiers inside, and two more in the cockpit. Kate saw with a sense of surprise that both pilots were women, as were two of the soldiers in the main cabin. They were occupied cleaning what looked like machine guns mounted inside two windows directly behind the pilot and copilot.

The pilot turned in her seat and gave Kate an appraising look before shifting her attention to Chase and the dog. A broad smile spread across her face. She extended her hand and offered the dog a treat, before shifting her attention back to Chase. "Hey, great to see you."

"Great to see you, too," he replied. "What have you been up to?"

"Keeping busy, doing the Afghan shuffle," she said with a grin. "When did you get back?"

"Yesterday."

Kate didn't miss how the other woman practically devoured Chase with her eyes, and she experienced an unfamiliar tightening in her chest at their obvious friendship.

"Let's catch up when we reach Camp Leatherneck," the pilot said, still smiling. "I have a lot to tell you."

"Yeah, I'd like that." Turning toward Kate, he indicated

one of the empty canvas jump seats. "Why don't you sit there and strap yourself in? We should be airborne in just a few minutes."

Kate did as he asked, fumbling briefly with the harness until Chase swept her hands aside and buckled her in himself. Kate told herself that her accelerated heart rate had to do with anticipation of the flight, and not with the way his hands brushed against her breasts. He took the seat next to her, and his hip pressed against hers in the narrow confines.

Kate watched as the two female soldiers slid the cabin doors closed and then took up positions at the open windows on either side of the cabin, their hands maneuvering the mounted machine guns with ease and confidence. Kate's stomach did an uneasy roll, and she was suddenly glad that she hadn't eaten breakfast. Glancing at the three male soldiers who sat in the other jump seats, Kate was relieved to see that none of them looked alarmed. In fact, one of them had tipped his head back against the seat and closed his eyes, apparently happy to sleep through the flight. Even Charity had settled down, curling up near Chase's seat with a small whine.

The pilot twisted in her seat and gave both Chase and Kate a smile. "Welcome aboard. I'm Captain Larson and your copilot today is Chief Warrant Officer Costanza. We'll be departing shortly. Our ETA at Camp Leatherneck is approximately 0900 hours. There's some adverse weather moving into the region, so the ride could get a little bumpy, but nothing to worry about." Her gaze touched briefly on Kate and then lingered on Chase. "Sit back and enjoy the flight."

The rotors whirred into life, and Kate forced herself to relax as she listened to the pilots go through their checklists for departure. Chase pulled a mobile device out of his pocket and began scrolling through his messages, as if he had no concerns at all. The action was so normal that Kate found herself relaxing in spite of herself.

"You okay?" he asked without looking at her.

"I think so. So the flight will take about two hours?"

"Give or take."

Even as he spoke, the enormous helicopter lifted from the ground. Through the window, Kate watched Bagram Airfield slide away beneath them. She found herself studying the two pilots and wondering what kind of woman would choose a career that endangered her life on a daily basis. Did Chase and Captain Larson have a romantic relationship? There was no question that the other woman was attractive, and Kate hadn't missed the way she looked at Chase, or how pleased he had been to see her.

"Will Tenley and her band also travel from Bagram to Camp Leatherneck in a helicopter?" she asked.

He glanced up briefly from his mobile device. "All of the singers and their band members will be transported in a Chinook. They're heavy-lift helicopters capable of transporting up to fifty-five people, so we should be able to get all of the performers in one trip, which means we have fewer helicopters tied up."

Kate tried to envision Tenley in a military helicopter but failed. She'd be scared to death. She couldn't picture her gentle sister over here, roughing it. How would she react to the sight of so many uniformed soldiers?

"Here, why don't you eat something?" Chase said, interrupting her thoughts.

Kate watched as he opened his rucksack and withdrew a large thermos and two cups. He poured them each a mug of steaming coffee and then passed the thermos to the other soldiers. Kate curled her fingers around the cup and inhaled the fragrance of the coffee.

"You had this in your backpack all this time and didn't tell me? Even though you knew I was dying for caffeine?"

Chase laughed softly and handed her a foil-wrapped Pop-Tart. "I can't have you thinking I'm a complete dick," he said, slanting her an amused look. "It's not a gourmet breakfast, but at least it's not an MRE." Reaching into the backpack, he withdrew a treat for Charity and let her eat it from his fingers, rubbing her head in approval when she took it gently.

Kate unwrapped the pastry and took a bite. "I haven't had a Pop-Tart since I was a kid."

They ate in silence, and Chase took her empty mug and wiped it clean before stowing it back in his rucksack. At that moment, the helicopter dipped sharply, and Kate would have come out of her seat if not for the harness. She gasped and reflexively clutched Chase's forearm.

"Relax," he soothed. "Just a little turbulence."

But when the helicopter suddenly dropped in altitude and shuddered violently, Kate saw that even the soldiers looked troubled. Charity lifted her head and gave a small whine, but Chase spoke to her gently and she dropped her muzzle back onto her paws. Instinctively, Kate clutched at Chase's hand, gratified when he didn't pull away.

"Are we crashing?" she asked, her heart slamming in her chest. "Maybe we should be wearing parachutes or something."

"Folks, we're encountering a storm front that's moving over the area," the copilot said over the intercom. "We're going to try and fly around it, but expect some turbulence."

"You see? Everything is fine," Chase said, and stretched his legs out and crossed his boots as if there was nothing to worry about.

Kate sat rigidly at his side, her fingers still curled in his, certain that he was wrong, that the pilots were only trying to avoid a panic in the cabin before they plummeted to the earth. Outside the windows, she could see the distant mountains and the dark storm clouds that had gathered on the horizon. She was only mildly comforted by the fact they were flying away from those mountains, and not directly into the storm.

"Try and get some sleep," Chase grunted. Pulling his hand free, he crossed his arms over his chest and dragged his baseball cap low over his eyes, effectively shutting her out.

Kate stared at him in disbelief. Even if she could relax enough to take a nap, the helmet and flak vest she wore made it nearly impossible to find a comfortable position. Her bottom ached from the angle of the jump seat, and the coffee and Pop-Tart sat heavily in her stomach. Looking around, she saw the other three soldiers had also closed their eyes, seemingly oblivious to the peril surrounding them.

With a deep breath, she sat back and tried to control her breathing, repeating her age-old mantra that when she had no control over the situation, she could at least control herself. But the flight took another nerve-racking two hours, where the helicopter occasionally bucked and dipped, and Kate only barely restrained herself from grabbing onto Chase again. It wasn't until they began to descend that he finally stirred and opened his eyes, looking rested and relaxed.

"Did you manage to get any sleep?" he asked innocently.

Kate gave him a baleful look, and then saw the telltale dimple in his cheek.

"You know I didn't," she said through gritted teeth.

"We'll be on the ground in just a few minutes," he said, glancing out the window.

Following his gaze, Kate saw another military base that looked remarkably like the one they had just left. "Are you sure we didn't just fly around in circles for two hours and land back at Bagram?" she asked doubtfully. Even the mountains on the horizon seemed exactly the same.

Chase chuckled. "I'm sure. Camp Leatherneck isn't nearly as big as Bagram, but the conditions are actually better. I may have to leave you for a bit while I secure accommodations for you."

Kate covered her mouth and yawned hugely. "As long as I can have another cup of coffee, I'll be fine." Reaching down, she patted her shoulder bag. "I have my book and my iPod."

They were met on the helipad by two soldiers in a Humvee. As they crossed the tarmac to the waiting vehicle, the wind tore at Kate's hair, dragging it loose from her ponytail and spraying sand against her exposed skin. Chase tried to shield her with his body, but the stinging wind was relentless.

"Oh, my God," she gasped when she was safely inside the Humvee. "Are we in a sandstorm?"

Chase tossed their luggage into the back of the vehicle and climbed in beside her. "No. If that was a sandstorm, you wouldn't be able to walk outside without face protection. This is just a storm front moving in. You can take off the helmet. Here, let me help you with the vest."

Chase deftly unfastened Kate's flak vest and helped her remove it. At the same time, the soldier driving the Humvee glanced at them in the rearview mirror. "We're due for some pretty nasty weather later this afternoon and through the night," he commented. "And you know what that means."

Kate looked at Chase in time to see him send the driver a silent warning with his eyes. "What does that mean?" she asked, a frisson of alarm feathering its way along her spine.

"There's a higher incidence of mortar attacks during bad weather," he said. "But I don't want you to worry. Even if we come under attack, the insurgents don't have the technology to direct their mortars with any accuracy."

Kate stared at him, appalled. "So a bomb could literally land anywhere on the base?"

"We have a good tracking system. The warning sirens will go off and we'll have time to get to a bunker." He tapped the helmet that lay on the seat between them. "But if you hear the sirens, make sure you don't go out without this."

Warning sirens? Kate knew her eyes had widened, but she hadn't really considered the possibility that they could come under attack. "What about you?" she asked. "If I have your protective gear, what are you going to wear?"

"We'll make a stop at the military supply office. They'll have a helmet and a flak vest that you can borrow while you're here, and we'll review the protocol for how to respond if the warning sirens should go off."

To hide her dismay, she stared out the window as they drove, pretending an interest in the buildings and military vehicles they passed. "Does that happen very often?" she finally managed, relieved that her voice didn't betray her inner fear.

"Not too often. As I said, we have a pretty good surveillance system set up on the perimeter, but a strike could occur at any time, so it's best to be prepared."

"Of course." She wondered what she would do if a strike happened during the night, when he wasn't with her? "So just where are these bunkers?"

"They're situated about every one hundred yards throughout the base," he assured her. "Don't look so worried. You'll be fine. I'm not going to leave you, so if anything should happen, I'll be right there with you."

That's what Kate was afraid of. She was more or less accustomed to being in the company of good-looking men, most of them associated with the music industry. But she wasn't used to having male attention focused on *her*. Most of the men she knew were only interested in how her association with Tenley could benefit them. Kate had simply been a means to an end, or completely invisible. Having Chase's full and undivided attention made her feel funny inside, as if she was either very fragile or very important. No man had ever acted as her protector before, or even indicated that he cared one way or the other about her well-being.

As the Humvee drove across the base, Chase pointed out various buildings along the way, including the base exchange store, a small post office, a recreation center and a fitness center.

"You seem pretty familiar with this place," Kate observed. "Do you spend a lot of time here?"

He shrugged. "This is my fourth tour. I've spent time on just about every U.S. base in the country at one time or another."

They pulled to a stop outside a large building constructed of corrugated metal, which Chase explained was the supply center. Inside, Kate saw it was really a warehouse filled with floor-to-ceiling shelves loaded with bins and bags. She followed Chase up and down the aisles as he selected items seemingly at random. Finally, when his arms were full, he made his way to a small window where a uniformed soldier dumped everything into a duffel bag and had him sign a hand-receipt.

"Think you can carry this?" Chase asked, handing her the duffel bag.

Kate took it from him, and nearly buckled under the weight. "What do you have in here?" she asked, grimacing. "Rocks?"

Reaching out, Chase took the bag from her as if it weighed nothing. "Your new protective gear." He grinned. "You won't be required to use it here unless we come under attack, but when we head to some of the FOBs, you'll need to wear it whenever you go outside."

They returned to the Humvee, and Kate watched as Chase stowed the duffel bag in the back of the vehicle. "What's an FOB?"

"A forward operating base. Those are the smaller bases that are essentially on the front lines, away from the central command centers. They don't have much in the way of amenities, which is why they really appreciate it when entertainers come out to visit them."

"Are FOBs dangerous?"

"They can be," he acknowledged. "Some more than others."

She digested his words silently, envisioning a primitive, fortresslike base surrounded by a perimeter of thick mud walls, sandbags and concertina wire, while terrorists lurked behind rocks and bushes, just waiting for the right moment to launch an attack.

"Having second thoughts?" he asked perceptively.

She tipped her chin up and met his eyes determinedly. "Of course not."

He studied her face for a long moment, and then raised a hand to briefly cup her cheek and rub his thumb over her jaw. "Good," he said.

As he climbed back into the Humvee, Kate put her fingers where his hand had been. In that instant, she understood that Chase Rawlins posed a greater danger to her than any mortars or insurgent attacks.

7

CHASE WANTED NOTHING MORE than to get Kate Fitzgerald settled in her own quarters so that he could get away from her, even for a few hours. No matter how he tried, he couldn't stop his imagination from retreating back to his housing unit at Bagram, and his bedroom, where he could once again envision her spread out beneath him. He hadn't meant to kiss her, but when she'd pressed her lips against his own, he'd been unable to resist her softness.

She'd smelled like sugar and vanilla and he'd wanted to consume her. He still couldn't believe he'd lost control the way he had. His only excuse was that he'd been in Afghanistan for way too long, away from everything soft and feminine and sexy. But goddamn, when he recalled how gorgeous she'd looked on his bed, with her luscious breasts in his hands, he grew aroused all over again. He could have taken her right then; could have used her welcoming body to satisfy his own raging desire.

But he didn't want her like that. He had nothing to offer any woman right now, not when he was committed to the Army and still had six months left of his current deployment. Kate didn't deserve to be used, and he wouldn't let himself take advantage of her, even if she thought it was what she wanted.

After he'd left her, he'd gone over to his command headquarters building, intending to catch up on the reports he was required to submit regarding the hunt for Al-Azir. But he'd been so distracted and aroused that he'd finally headed across to the fitness center and worked out his frustration on the treadmill and weight machines. Then he'd found himself in front of his housing unit just before dawn, imagining Kate inside, sleeping in his bed. He'd been tempted to go in and wake her up and finish what they'd started, but common sense had overcome his libido.

For the first time, he wished he could be more like his twin brother, Chance, who never passed up an opportunity to get busy with an attractive woman. At least, he used to be like that. Now Chance was fully committed to the pretty Black Hawk pilot, Jenna Larson, who had flown them from Bagram to Camp Leatherneck. They weren't talking marriage—at least not yet—but Chase knew there was no way his brother was going to let Jenna get away. He was happy for both of them, but he wasn't looking for something similar. He didn't need to complicate his life with a relationship that had zero chance of going anywhere, no matter how appealing he might find Kate.

When he'd first learned that he would escort her to each of the bases, he'd contacted the USO at Camp Leatherneck and had learned that Kate could stay in the tent designated for the other performers. Chase suspected it would be very much like the one at Bagram Air Base, only this time there would be no other women bunking with her; she would be completely alone. Since he didn't have his own housing unit on Camp Leatherneck, Chase wouldn't have the option of letting her sleep in his quarters.

As he suspected, the Humvee drew to a stop in front of a

large tent, nearly identical to the one at Bagram. The wind had picked up and buffeted the canvas sides, causing them to billow out and suck back in. Kate stared out the window and Chase was unable to read her expression.

Climbing out of the Humvee, he opened the back and whistled to Charity, who bounded down and began exploring the area around the tent. He grabbed Kate's duffel bag and waited for her to join him.

"Why do I have a bad feeling about this?" she asked. The wind picked up tendrils of her hair and blew them across her mouth, and Chase had to resist the urge to brush them away with his finger.

"I doubt there's much difference between these accommodations and where you stayed at Bagram," he said reasonably. "I spoke to the woman over at the USO, who said this is where all the entertainers will stay while they're here."

He pushed through the entrance of the tent, sensing Kate directly behind him. The tent was larger than the one at Bagram, with at least three dozen bunk beds lined up along the walls. The USO staff had hung curtains between the bunks in an effort to provide some privacy. But where the other tent had been sparsely outfitted, this tent was equipped with metal lockers and several small refrigerators. Chase set the duffel bag down inside the door and turned to look at Kate.

"Please tell me you're joking," she finally said, turning to him. "There is absolutely no way that Tenley can stay here." She gave a disbelieving laugh and gestured toward the cots. "She's the only female in her band! Are you actually suggesting she sleep here with a bunch of guys, with only a scrap of material separating her from them?"

Chase crossed his arms. "Well, she'll have you to protect her."

"No way. There must be somewhere else. What about

the time Carrie Underwood visited? Are you telling me that she stayed here?"

"No. She stayed in a private housing unit, but unfortunately we don't have any available at the present time." He gestured around him. "This is the alternative, and if it's adequate for the other performers, I have to believe it's adequate for you and your sister."

Kate blew out a hard breath. "I knew the conditions over here would be harsh, but to have her sleep in the same tent with a dozen guys?" She gave Chase a helpless look. "Really, Chase? There's nothing else available?"

"Is she in any danger from her own band?"

He could see Kate considering this before she shook her head. "No, but it's not…appropriate. The point is, she shouldn't *have* to bunk with her band. She's an impressionable young girl, and she should have her own private accommodations. Wait…" She turned and stared at him. "Did you say I'm also staying here?"

"I did."

Chase watched her expression turn from dismay to horror.

"Am I supposed to sleep here tonight? Alone?"

Oh, man. He knew her words weren't an invitation, but he couldn't prevent his imagination from surging.

"Unfortunately, I don't have my own private housing unit for you to crash in," he said.

Kate's gaze locked with his and awareness flared in her eyes. Chase knew she was remembering what had happened between them, and when her lips parted on a soft "oh," he realized he had to leave. He couldn't stop thinking about the previous night, and now it seemed he couldn't stop talking about it, either.

"You'll be fine," he assured her. "Let's go over and check out the concert venue, and then grab some lunch."

He glanced outside. "This storm is going to be here before dark, so we should go soon."

"Before we do that, is there someone at the USO that I can talk to?" She gave him a pleading look. "You don't know Tenley. She'll be miserable if she has to stay here."

"Kate, trust me when I say I do understand. But this isn't Bagram Air Base, and they just don't have the resources here that Bagram has." He gestured toward the metal bunk beds with one hand. "This is what's available, and I'm sorry if it's not up to your usual standards, but it's what you get."

Blowing out a breath, she picked up her pink duffel bag and dropped it onto the nearest bunk. "For myself, I don't really care where I sleep. But Tenley deserves better."

Chase found his resolve crumbling beneath her obvious distress. At the same time, he couldn't help but admire how doggedly she looked out for her sister.

"Okay, look," he said, scrubbing a hand across the back of his neck. "Let's go over and talk to the USO folks. Maybe they can figure out alternate arrangements for the two of you." She gave him a grateful smile, and he raised a hand to forestall the words of gratitude that he knew hovered on her lips. "Just don't get your hopes up. They may not have anything else to offer you. When I talked with them, it sounded like they were stretched pretty thin."

Kate made a sound of frustration and sat down heavily on the bunk. "I don't know why I came over here," she lamented softly. "What was I thinking? Russell tried to talk me out of this, but I thought it was our only chance to save Tenley's career."

Chase had no idea who Russell was, but he felt a surge of jealousy that Kate somehow relied on this man. Worse, it sounded as if she was on the verge of tears. He could handle her anger and her indignation, but he wasn't sure how he would deal with her tears.

"Okay, c'mon," he relented. "Let's go over to the USO and then we'll take a quick look at the concert venue, okay?"

Kate didn't meet his eyes, but she nodded. "Okay." Her voice was subdued.

Chase frowned. Was she crying? He was torn between wanting to go to her, and wanting to run as fast as he could in the opposite direction. In the end, cowardice won out and he retreated toward the exit.

"I'll wait for you outside," he said.

The Humvee had departed. Chase would spend the night bunking with a Marine Corps battalion, and had given the Humvee driver instructions to drop his protective gear and duffel bag off at their tent. Now he wondered if he hadn't been a little hasty in sending the guys off. The wind was still blowing, and the small rocks and dust that it kicked up made it unpleasant to be outside for any length of time. When Kate finally emerged from the tent, she looked composed, but resolute.

"All set?" he asked.

She nodded. "Yes."

She didn't say anything else, and Chase didn't ask. He was just relieved that she wasn't crying. He could pretty much deal with anything, but not tears.

"The USO office is about a ten-minute walk from here," he said as she fell into step beside him. The wind was at their back, so they avoided the worst of the debris that was flying around. But when they finally reached the office, they were both covered in a fine coating of dust. The USO was housed in a large, one-floor building and consisted of a lounge equipped with oversize leather chairs, flat-screened televisions and a bank of computers and telephones. At least a dozen soldiers were sprawled in the chairs watching television, or sat at the computers, connecting with family members and friends back home. Chase could see two civilians inside the office, and pointed them out to Kate.

"Do you want me to come with you when you talk with them?"

"No, I can take it from here. This is what I do."

Chase sat down in a chair where he had a clear view of the office, and watched as Kate went in and closed the door behind her. Through the glass windows that separated the office from the public lounge, he could see her negotiating with the two USO representatives. She had her little planner with her, and was busy taking notes as she talked with the women. They were smiling and nodding, and she reached into her oversize shoulder bag and withdrew what looked like a handful of oversize glossy photos of Tenley Miles. She handed one to each woman. They spoke for several more minutes, and then Kate came out, looking extremely pleased with herself.

Chase rose to his feet. "All set?"

She smiled at him and tucked her planner into her bag. "They're going to provide a semi-private housing unit for Tenley when she arrives. She'll stay in a unit with me and two other women, but at least she won't have to sleep in the tent with the band members."

Chase had to give her credit. He had talked with the USO representatives in the hours before Kate had arrived and had been told in no uncertain terms that the only option was for her to stay in the tent.

"I'm impressed," he said to her as they left the building.

She gave him an arch smile. "It's amazing what a little bit of charm can get you. You should try it some time."

He grinned. "Didn't you notice? This is me at my most charming."

To his relief, she laughed. "Yeah, right."

"So where are you staying tonight?" he asked. "I'll make sure your gear gets moved to the new location."

"Unfortunately, it looks like I'll be in that tent by myself until the performers arrive. Then the two women at the USO are giving up their own beds for Tenley and me."

"Really? And where will they stay?"

Kate shrugged. "They said they can put some cots in the USO office and sleep there for a couple of nights."

"And you're okay with that? You don't mind displacing other people for your own convenience?"

Kate gave him a level look. "Not for my own convenience, for Tenley's. And it's not as if they'll be sleeping outside. They offered to do this. I didn't ask them to."

Chase didn't know why he should feel so disappointed, but he did. He admired the fact that she would go to any length to ensure her sister's safety and comfort, but he didn't like how easily she could disrupt other people's lives to do so.

"Does she have any idea that people bend over backwards to accommodate her, or does she just expect it?"

He watched as Kate drew in a deep breath, and then stopped to face him. "If you have a problem with this, Major Rawlins, maybe you should assign somebody else to escort me around. This is why I came over here—to make sure Tenley has everything she needs. She has no idea how much work goes into preparing for a concert. Like I said before, she's just a kid. She has enough to contend with, without having to worry about the logistics of where she is going to eat, sleep, etc. That's my job."

Charity gave a soulful whimper, as if sensing the tension between them.

"Okay, then," Chase said. "Let's go over and make sure the concert site meets with your approval."

They walked in silence after that. As much as Chase was

attracted to Kate, he couldn't help but think this assignment was a waste of his time. She could clearly take care of herself. Meanwhile, part of his team was up in the mountains doing his job for him. He wondered how they were doing, and how soon he could rejoin them.

Beside him, Kate's shoulders were rigidly set and she stared straight ahead. Even as they toured the staging area where the bands would perform, she pointedly ignored him. She made some notes in her planner, and examined where the bands would wait backstage, but didn't give him any indication of whether she approved of the site or not. But he'd seen Kate's face when she'd thought Tenley would have to stay with the other band members, and he knew that her misgivings stemmed from a true concern for her sister.

After viewing the concert venue, they walked over to the dining facility and had lunch. But unlike the day before, there was no small talk. They might have been complete strangers for all the attention Kate paid him. Chase tried several times to make conversation with her, but after receiving short, polite responses, he gave up. He told himself that if she wanted to keep him at arm's length, then he was fine with that. In another week she would be gone. He had no desire to get to know Kate Fitzgerald. He told himself for the hundredth time that she was simply an assignment, and once that assignment was over, he could get back to what he should have been doing all along: hunting and capturing Al-Azir.

This was exactly why he avoided women and tried not to encourage those who did show an interest in him; they were a distraction. Even now, when he should be spending his spare time coordinating with his team members and laying out a plan for their continued pursuit of Al-Azir, he found his thoughts consumed by Kate. He needed to get away from her, even if it was just for a couple of hours. He wondered if his brother was at Camp Leatherneck.

Chance was an Apache helicopter pilot, and his missions took him to many of the U.S. bases, although he was stationed at Bagram. But it hadn't escaped Chase's notice that his brother somehow managed to fly into Camp Leatherneck about once every two weeks, and it was no coincidence that the trips just happened to coincide with those times that Captain Jenna Larson was also at Camp Leatherneck. On second thought, he decided that even if his brother was on the base, Chase was unlikely to get any quality time with him. Chance would be fully occupied with Jenna.

He watched Kate eat her lunch. Although she deliberately ignored him, Chase could see that she was acutely aware of him. She watched him when she thought he didn't notice, and she was attuned to every movement he made. He hadn't been in his line of business for nearly eight years without being able to read body language, and everything about Kate screamed awareness of him.

He couldn't believe the difference a day made. Just yesterday, he'd been chomping at the bit to return to the field and resume his hunt for Al-Azir. Now, for the first time in years, he wasn't thinking about duty and country. With a sense of dismay, he realized he wanted more.

He wanted Kate Fitzgerald.

8

ON A PRETEXT OF having business to attend to, Chase left Kate at the USO for the afternoon. He needed some time to get his head together and put things in perspective. Colonel Decker had made it clear that his only mission for the next week was to take care of Kate and her sister, but he also needed to touch base with the rest of his team. Even if the stand-down order was lifted in the next day or so, he was committed to remaining with Kate until the tour had ended.

Kate seemed happy at the prospect of spending time at the USO. She would have internet and phone access, and had insisted she needed to reach both Tenley and Russell. He'd desperately wanted to know if Russell was a boyfriend, but pride prevented him from asking. They had agreed that he would return to collect her after dinner. The dining facility was located directly next door to the USO, so she didn't need an escort. He felt a little disgruntled by the fact that she seemed happy at the prospect of eating a meal alone. She hadn't talked about staying in the large tent by herself, but the more Chase thought about it, the less he liked the idea, especially with a storm moving into the region. He'd already made up his mind to hunker down outside the entrance for the night, just in case she needed him. He'd slept in worse places, in worse conditions, so the idea didn't faze him.

By the time Chase jogged over to the USO to get Kate, the temperatures had dropped significantly, and the wind had kicked up a notch. Dust whipped across the ground in swirling clouds, and he could hear the patter of tiny stones as they clattered against the metal buildings. In the distance, flashes of lightning briefly illuminated the mountain peaks.

The storm was rolling in quickly, and it promised to be a good one. Kate was waiting for him by the entrance, her enormous shoulder bag over one arm. Even in the dim light he could see the apprehension on her face as she looked toward the northwest.

"C'mon," he said briskly, "let's get you back to your tent before the rain starts." He indicated the road, which was packed dirt and rocks. "You don't want to be out here once the ground gets wet."

"Is there any chance I can take a shower before I turn in?" she asked hopefully.

Chance had already planned on hitting the showers after he dropped her off at her tent, so it would be no big deal to walk her over to the bathrooms. "Absolutely," he assured her. "I'll leave you at your tent while I go and grab my own gear, and then come back for you."

The wind kept her from responding, so she just nodded and then put her head down. She kept pace with him as they walked quickly across the base. On the left, he pointed out the nearest bunker, illuminated by an orange safety light. The exterior of the concrete bunker was packed high with sandbags.

"There's another shelter just beyond the bathrooms," he said, drawing her close and raising his voice to be heard over the wind. "If the sirens go off while you're in the shower, use that bunker instead."

He left her at her own tent and then quickly jogged to the Marine battalion quarters, and stuffed a clean uniform and his shower gear into his backpack. Other soldiers were running to reach their destinations before the storm hit, and Chase looked to the sky, trying to estimate how much time they might have before the heavens opened up. They didn't often get storm fronts of this magnitude in southern Afghanistan, and when they did, they usually took the form of sandstorms. But he already knew that this particular storm was packing a lot of moisture, and the troops were battening down the hatches in preparation for a significant amount of rain. He knew that Kate would be okay; her tent had been erected on top of a wooden platform, so she would be safe from flooding. But the tents were prone to seepage, and there was a good chance that she would have several leaks during the course of the night.

It was almost completely dark by the time he returned to Kate's tent and found her waiting for him just inside the entrance. They jogged the short distance to the bathroom, not wanting to get caught in the threatening downpour.

Chase stepped into the entry with Kate. "I'll be right next door," he assured her. "Wait for me here. I'll give you a shout when I'm ready to walk you back to the tent, got it?"

Kate nodded. "I'll be quick."

"Okay, fine. I'll be back in ten minutes to get you."

Ducking into the men's showers, on the opposite side of the same building, Chase quickly stripped down and stepped under the steaming water, grateful to scrub away the dust and grit from the base. Since it was still the dinner hour, he had the entire facility to himself. He could easily have stayed under the hot water for hours, but sensitive to the fact that Kate would be waiting for him, he rinsed the soap from his skin and turned off the tap. Then, wrapping a towel around his hips, he stood over a sink and used a razor to scrape the

beard growth from his jaw and neck. Scrutinizing his reflection, he decided he still looked rough around the edges,
but at least he no longer resembled a mercenary.

He was wiping the last traces of shaving cream from his
jaw when the lights in the bathroom flickered. Outside, he
could hear the wind whistling across the base. The doors
rattled on their hinges. Chase turned swiftly toward the stall
where he had left his gear and a clean change of clothing,
but he was too late. The lights flickered once more, omi-
nously, before they went out, plunging the bathroom into
utter darkness.

Abandoning his clothing, Chase made a beeline for the
door, bolting through it and into the windy darkness outside. He knew it would only be a minute or two before the
lights came back on or the backup generators kicked in, but
he didn't want Kate to panic.

He burst through the doors of the women's bathrooms,
calling her name. "Kate? Are you okay? It's me, Chase."

He heard her footsteps stumble toward him, and then she
was in his arms, her hands groping blindly at him.

"Chase?" He could hear the surprise in her voice. "What
are you doing in here? Isn't there some rule against— Are
you *naked?*"

Her fingers encountered his bare torso, and before he
could stop them, they skittered over his shoulders and
arms, drawing heat to the surface of his skin wherever they
touched. Grasping her wrists, he dragged her hands away.

"No," he snapped in irritation at himself and his body's
reaction to her. "I am *not* naked. I was just getting dressed
when the power went out. I didn't want you to be frightened,
so I ran over. The backup generators should—" There was an
audible click, then a buzz of electricity, and the emergency
lights over the doors snapped on, illuminating the bathroom

in an eerie red glow. "Kick in any second," Chase finished, his voice trailing off as he got a good look at Kate.

As lights went, they weren't much, but they were more than sufficient for him to see that she wore nothing but a pair of underpants and a bra, and his mouth went dry at the sight. He'd been right about one thing—she had curves in all the right places. Her hips flared out from a narrow waist, and her legs were slim and supple.

"Oh, my God," she breathed, her eyes widening as they traveled over him. For just an instant, Chase saw female appreciation and raw hunger in her expression, and in the next instant she spun away to snatch a towel from the nearby sink and hold it against her. "I'm fine, really," she said over her shoulder. "You can go now and—and put some clothes on."

Chase stood there for a moment, dumbstruck. Despite the fact that he'd already seen her partially nude and knew she had a gorgeous shape, he was blown away by the entire package. Even her back was lovely, and he took a second to admire the elegant line of her spine and the deep curves of her waist. Her rear was luscious and rounded, and he had an instant image of himself cupping her cheeks in his hands and driving himself into her warmth as she straddled his hips. Then he gave himself a mental shake. He was losing it, big-time.

"I'll see you in a few minutes," he muttered, and returned to the men's side of the shower facilities, his head still reeling.

For as long as Chase could recall, women had been attracted to him and his identical twin, Chance. But where Chance had welcomed every feminine advance and had been considered something of a player, Chase had been completely focused on his future as a Special Ops commando. He'd known from an early age that he wanted to join the elite unit, and nothing—not even a pretty face and a curvy body—could deter him from that path. He'd had girlfriends, but none of them had been more important to him than achieving his goal.

In fact, looking back, he realized he'd deliberately kept women at a distance because he'd known his dedication to the Army would prevent him from committing himself fully to a relationship. But right now, with his body aroused from just seeing her, he thought he would gladly trade his entire freaking career for just one night with Kate Fitzgerald.

Yeah, he'd definitely lost it.

Pulling on a clean uniform, Chase stuffed his dirty gear into his backpack, telling himself that he'd have no problem facing Kate. He'd seen plenty of women with less clothing on than the scraps of fabric she'd been wearing, and he'd never been so overcome by lust that he'd lost his self-control. He'd just keep it professional and act like he hadn't seen anything. Like he hadn't cupped and caressed her breasts less than twenty-four hours earlier. Like he had no idea how her nipple felt in his mouth, against his tongue, or how her small sounds of pleasure drove him crazy.

Yeah, right.

Bracing himself, he stepped outside. Rain was just beginning to fall in big, fat drops, and the sky flashed with lightning mere seconds before a roll of thunder caused the ground to tremble beneath his boots. He pulled a small flashlight out of his backpack and flicked it on, not because he couldn't find his way back, or because he couldn't see in the dark, but because he knew it would give Kate a sense of security. Standing just outside the door to the women's showers, he called her name.

She came out immediately, although Chase didn't miss how she avoided his eyes, concentrating instead on adjusting her bag over her shoulder. But when the first raindrops hit her face, she blinked in surprise and lifted a hand to catch several.

"Wow, this storm is moving in fast," she observed.

"They usually do out here," Chase replied. "We'd better hurry, or we'll find ourselves soaked to the skin before we reach your tent. Here, let me take your bag."

Ignoring her protests, he took the shoulder bag from her and slid a hand beneath her elbow. He sensed her surprise, but she didn't try to pull away. The rain was coming down in sheeting torrents now, mixing with the dusty road and creating mud that had the consistency of peanut butter. It sucked at his feet with every step, and if it weren't for the fact that his boots were laced up over his ankles, they might have been pulled free.

Kate wasn't so lucky.

She gave a small cry of distress and stumbled heavily, pulling Chase to an abrupt halt. He steadied her as she leaned her weight against him and balanced herself on one foot. Swiping the water from his face, Chase looked down to see one of her slip-on shoes buried in the muck. He pulled it free, and she grimaced as she pushed her foot back into it.

"So much for that shower," she shouted.

Chase peered up at the sky. "Yeah, well, you don't know the meaning of the word *shower* until you've experienced a desert storm. This is just going to get worse. C'mon."

But no sooner did they take another step, than Kate's other shoe became stuck in the mud. Chase flicked his light over the ground, seeing the water pooling quickly around Kate's foot. She could put the shoe back on, but he already knew they'd be retrieving her footwear from the mud with every step she took. The way he saw it, they had two choices: she could go barefoot all the way back to her sleeping quarters, or he could carry her. He told himself firmly that the thought of holding her in his arms for the five-minute trek did not send his pulse into overdrive.

"Okay, listen," he said, using his best authoritative voice, "I'm going to carry you back to the tent, otherwise we'll be playing hop-along the whole way."

She stared up at him, and in the beam from the flashlight, her lashes were spiky with moisture, and rivulets of water streamed down her face and slicked her hair to her scalp. She blinked furiously.

"You can't carry me," she protested. "First of all, I weigh a ton, and second of all, it's not necessary. I'll just go barefoot."

"No, that's not an option," he said briskly. "The road is loaded with stones and potholes. If you don't end up with a serious laceration, you could twist an ankle. Just let me carry you. You don't weigh a ton, trust me. I carry seventy pounds of equipment on my back whenever I'm in the field."

She gave him a tolerant look. "I weigh a little more than seventy pounds."

Chase handed her the shoulder bag. "Here, carry this. Now put your arms around my neck."

A brilliant flash of lightning, followed by a low boom of thunder, caused her to clutch his arm, and Chase took advantage of her startled reaction, bending down to slide an arm behind her knees. He lifted her effortlessly, and the thought flashed through his head that she really didn't weigh much more than seventy pounds. She turned her face into his neck as he strode along the muddy road, and even with the rain lashing against his face, he could smell her soap and shampoo. Her breath came in warm pants against his skin, and he arrived at her tent much too quickly. He set her down just inside the entrance.

"I lost my shoe back there," she said.

Chase looked down at her bare, mud-covered foot. "I'll

go back and get it," he offered. "Here, take my flashlight. The power's out, so the lights won't work in here. There's bottled water and some towels at the back of the tent that you can use to clean up."

"What about you?" she asked. "How will you see anything?"

He pulled out a second, smaller flashlight from a pocket on his camo pants. "Always ready," he said with a quick grin. "I'll be right back."

She nodded, swiping moisture from her face. "Okay, thanks."

Chase sprinted back the way they had come until he found her shoe. It was a flat-soled, cloth shoe that might have been blue or purple, but right now it was coated in a thick, yellowish mud. Wiping the worst of it off, he jogged back to the tent. Kate had put the flashlight on the small side table next to her bunk bed and stood toweling her hair dry. In the instant before she knew he was there, he saw the weariness on her face and in the droop of her slender shoulders. Her clothes were soaking wet and plastered to her skin. He cleared his throat and she turned toward him, smoothing her features into an expression of pleasant expectation. She grimaced when she saw the sopping shoe in his hand.

"Maybe I should just consider these shoes as collateral damage and throw them away."

"Leave them outside the tent and let the rain wash them clean," Chase suggested. "Once the sun comes out, they'll be dry within minutes."

Another bolt of lightning flashed brilliance behind him, followed by a sharp crack of thunder. Kate didn't jump, but Chase saw how she clutched the towel convulsively in her hands. He intended to spend the night just outside her tent, in case she needed him, but if Kate found out she would protest.

"Okay, listen, I'm going back to my tent to change into

dry clothes and grab my rain gear, and then I'll come check on you," he said. "If you want, we can play cards or something. I can hang out here until the worst of the storm passes."

She looked relieved. "I'd like that, thanks."

He turned to go, but her voice halted him.

"You're coming right back?" He could hear the anxiety in her voice.

"I'll be gone for less than ten minutes," he assured her. "Why don't you get out of those wet clothes and get warm?"

He knew she felt apprehensive about being alone in the big tent, and now he wished that he had tried to find her other accommodations until her client arrived. He told himself it was only for one night. Tomorrow, they would view the first concert venue in the morning and then drive to Kandahar, where the USO had arranged for the third and final concert. By the time they returned to Bagram two days later, Tenley Miles would have arrived. The performers would spend five days giving concerts and meeting the troops, then they would fly back to the States and Kate Fitzgerald would go with them. Two days ago he'd been resentful at the prospect of babysitting the publicist. Now he realized that he didn't want her to leave.

KATE WAITED UNTIL Chase left, then secured the entrance to the tent as best she could. The wind still whistled outside and the rain drummed against the roof. Chase had made the interior seem almost cozy with his height and broad shoulders, but now it seemed big and empty. The flashlight illuminated the area directly around her bunk, but the rest of the large tent was cast in dark shadows that undulated with the wind and rain and made her think that someone was on the other side of the canvas, trying to get in.

Shivering, she opening her duffel bag and pulled out a

pair of flannel lounge pants and a loose top. The walls of the tent sucked noisily in and out with the force of the wind, and Kate wished Chase would hurry. Fishing in her pocket, she pulled out the beeper that he had given to her earlier, and closed her fingers over it. Just holding it made her feel marginally better. She wanted to push it, but then he would know what a complete fraud she was, and that everything about this trip totally freaked her out. Besides, he'd promised that he would be right back; what would she say to him when he arrived? That she was afraid of the dark? That she was afraid of being alone? That he made her feel safe?

Yeah, right. If only that was all he made her feel. She recalled how he had looked in the bathroom, with nothing but a towel wrapped around his hips. His body was layered with lean muscle and sculpted to masculine perfection. He was hot enough to bake cookies on. She could still picture the thrust of his broad shoulders and the bulging biceps in his powerful arms. She remembered again the feel of his mouth on her breast, and how perfectly he'd fitted in the cradle of her hips.

Just the memory of his body caused something to fist low in her stomach. Most of the time, he looked at her as if she was an annoyance, or just another mission that he needed to complete successfully. He'd said the incident in his bedroom had been a mistake, but for those few moments in the bathroom, she had seen something else in his eyes. Something hot and needy. Something that had caused a rush of heat beneath her skin.

Shivering, she realized the temperature had dropped dramatically from what it had been earlier in the day. Chase hadn't exaggerated when he'd said the nights could get cold. Quickly, she stripped out of her wet clothing and changed into the flannel lounge pants and top, and pulled on a pair of socks. Still, she couldn't get warm. She shook out the sleeping bag that had been left at the foot of the cot and unzipped it, dragging it around her shoulders like a shawl. But even cocooned in its warmth, she couldn't stop shivering.

The flap of the tent billowed and then Chase was there, bringing the wind and rain with him, until he secured the entrance. Shrugging out of his rain poncho, he hung it from a support beam and turned toward Kate just as a crack of thunder sounded overhead.

Chase grinned. "I can't remember the last time I saw a storm like this over here. Are you okay?"

Kate nodded, relieved to have him there. "Are you sure it's safe to be in a tent? What if it gets struck by lightning?"

Chase sat down on the bed directly beside hers, leaning forward to link his hands between his knees. For the first time, Kate noticed that he had shaved his beard, revealing the strong, square line of his jaw. She wanted to stroke her fingers over the smooth skin.

"The tents are grounded," he said, "so you have nothing to worry about. More than half of the troops on this base live in tents, and we haven't lost one in a storm yet."

The rain thundered on the canvas roof, and Kate pulled the sleeping bag a little closer around her shoulders. "I guess I'll just have to trust you."

An odd expression crossed his face, and Kate was surprised when he stood up. "Right. Which is why I should leave. Try to get some sleep."

"What?" Pushing the sleeping bag off, Kate stood up and followed him across the tent. "Why are you leaving? I thought you were going to stay, at least until the storm passes."

Chase paused in the act of retrieving his rain gear and gave her a disbelieving look. "Kate, if I stay here with you, do you really believe we'll play cards?"

Kate's breath caught at the expression on his face, and her heart leaped in her chest. "Look, if it's about last night—"

"Yes, damn it, it is about last night." His voice was a low growl. He leaned forward until his face was just inches from hers and raked her with a heated look. "I'm trying very hard to keep this professional, but every time I look at you, I see you lying across my bed, making little gasping sounds as I touch you. Christ…" He spun halfway around and scrubbed a hand over his hair before turning back to her. "So just—give me a break, okay? Understand that this has nothing with my not wanting to stay with you. I *can't* stay with you. Not unless you want to be flat on your back in that bunk with me inside you."

His words caused Kate's heart to stop beating and then explode into overdrive. Part of her realized she should be at least a little bit frightened by this man, but the images he conjured up filled her with a buzz of awareness and a sense of her own feminine power. She knew that her eyes grew wide and her mouth fell open, but nobody had ever spoken to her so bluntly, or admitted that he wanted her enough that he couldn't trust himself to be with her.

Misreading her expression, Chase gave a rueful laugh.

"Pretty pathetic, huh? I guess I really have been deployed for too long."

Kate didn't know how to respond to that. Was it pathetic that he should find her attractive? And did he only find her attractive because he'd been deployed for so many months? How would he react if she told him that she hadn't been with a guy in almost two years? Now *that* was pathetic.

Outside, another flash of lightning illuminated the sky, and wind gusted through the entrance, bringing a spray of cold rain with it. Chase grabbed his poncho from the hook and dropped it over his head.

"You have my beeper," he said curtly. "Use it if you need me."

Kate stared at him in dismay, unable to comprehend that he was really going to leave her alone in the enormous tent while a storm raged outside. It was wrong to expect him to stay with her. She was a grown woman, after all, but she couldn't deny that she wanted him with her. "I don't need your damned beeper, Chase. I want *you*."

Chase held up a finger and gave her a warning look. "Don't. I'm barely holding it together here, Kate."

Before she could argue further, he pushed aside the flap and vanished into the night. Kate stood staring after him in disbelief for a full minute, expecting that he would reappear. But when an ear-splitting crack of thunder reverberated through the tent, Kate dashed back to her bunk and dragged the sleeping bag over her.

With her back pressed against the headboard, she sat with the flashlight in her hands, directing the beam at the entrance, certain that someone—or something—was going to get her before the night was over. The shadows seemed to grow and move in the corners, and the combined cacophony of rocks and sand being flung against the sides of the tent, as well as the hard rain drumming against the roof, guaranteed that she wouldn't get any sleep that night.

She realized she still clutched Chase's beeper in her hand, but nothing would induce her to press that button now. Not when he'd made it clear that he couldn't be alone with her. He obviously was a man of honor, and there was no way she would ask him to compromise his principles for her.

An ear-splitting crack of thunder directly overhead, followed by what sounded like an explosion very close by, made her jump with alarm. Drawing a deep breath, she pressed the beeper.

9

CHASE SAT JUST OUTSIDE the entrance of Kate's tent, hugging his poncho around his body, not that it did any good. The sheeting rain found its way inside the protective gear, and his clothing was soaked. Charity had refused to leave him, so he'd let her curl up beneath his poncho, but even she was dripping wet.

Beneath his feet, the ground was a swirling soup of red mud and rocks, and the wind caused the fabric of the tent to snap loudly. Reluctant to leave Kate alone, he had taken up watch for the night, just in case she needed him. The conditions were so bad that only the security vehicles were out, driving slowly through the flooded roads, their emergency lights cutting orange swaths through the wind and rain. Chase doubted there would be any chance of a mortar attack tonight, since the weather would drive even the insurgents for cover.

His tent was only a five-minute jog away, but he didn't want to risk anything happening to Kate in these conditions. The main power was still out, although the emergency lights were working. As he crouched by the entrance, a bolt of lightning lit up the sky, so close that he could feel the electricity in the air. The streak was followed immediately by a deafening crack of thunder, and a loud popping sound as the lightning struck a nearby transformer and caused it to explode, plunging the area into total darkness.

Chase pushed himself to his feet just as the beeper in his pocket began to vibrate. *Kate.* Making his way through the entrance of the tent, he stood just inside and swept the interior with his flashlight, looking for her. He found her huddled on the nearest bunk, wrapped in her sleeping bag and clutching the flashlight that he had given to her earlier.

"Are you okay?" he asked. He didn't come any closer. Water streamed down the rubber coating of his rain gear in heavy rivulets and pooled on the floor.

"How did you get here so quickly?" she asked. "I heard a noise, like an explosion, and it sounded pretty close."

"Yeah, the lightning took out a transformer just down the road."

In the indistinct light, he could see the speculation on her face as she considered him. "Were you standing outside my tent this whole time?"

"Just doing my job," he said evenly. "I meant what I said earlier—*attached at the hip.*"

Oh, man, if only. His words conjured up images that he had no business thinking about. Shaking off the disturbing thoughts, he strove for a professional tone.

"If you're okay, then I'll let you get some sleep. I'll be right outside if you need me." He turned to go.

"Wait!"

Chase stopped and looked at her expectantly. Another bolt of lightning flashed outside the tent, followed by a loud boom. To his surprise, Kate stood up, letting the sleeping bag fall onto the mattress. Her flannel pajama bottoms rode low on her hips, exposing a pale strip of skin along her abdomen. He swallowed hard and watched her approach, half hopeful, half filled with dread.

"As much as I appreciate you standing watch," she said, stopping just beyond the puddle of water he was creating, "I wouldn't put a dog out in these conditions." She looked pointedly at Charity, who stood in the doorway with her head down, shivering. "Not even a guard dog."

Chase hoped the hood of his poncho, combined with the darkness, hid his expression, because he knew he was eating her alive with his eyes. She looked warm and feminine and he ached to slide his hands into the back of her loose pajama bottoms and cup her luscious rear. He wanted to bend her over his arm and shove her shirt up so that he could lick her breasts. He couldn't remember when he'd had such a strong reaction to a woman, and he took a step back.

Kate hugged her arms around her middle, her expression one of concern. "Why don't you come in and dry off?"

"No, thanks. I'll just get wet again when I go back out."

"Look," she said, and Chase knew she tried to sound casual, but the way she rubbed her palms over her thighs told him she was nervous. "I'm not asking you to sleep with me, okay? But I'd feel safer if you were inside the tent with me. And since you're going to stand watch anyway, doesn't it make more sense to come in out of the rain?" She indicated a folding chair in the corner. "You can just as easily sit inside the entrance as you can outside, right?"

Chase rubbed a hand over his face. She'd never know how tempting her words were, but he had to admit that everything she said made sense. But he hadn't completely lost it. He still had a small vestige of brain cells left that functioned, warning him to retreat.

"General order number one prohibits any service member from entering the sleeping quarters of the opposite sex," he finally responded. "I shouldn't come inside."

"Well, I'm not a service member," she pointed out, "and surely allowances can be made for the fact that the weather is so terrible and all the power is out. You'd be able to do your job better if you were inside the tent. Besides, it's not like anyone is going to come out here in this weather to check on me—or you."

Still, he hesitated.

"Didn't you tell me that your job is to ensure my safety while I'm here?" she pressed. "That you are my single point of contact for everything, and that I don't do anything without you? If you refuse to do this, I will go to your commanding officer and tell him—"

"Okay, okay," Chase relented, interrupting her tirade. As threats went, hers was pretty ineffectual. As long as he kept Kate safe, his commanding officer had no interest in what he did or didn't do with her. He just hoped he wasn't making a huge mistake. "I'll bunk down inside the entrance, if you don't mind."

KATE FELT SOMETHING uncurl inside her at his words. No, she didn't mind in the least, and she stepped back to allow him to pass. Immediately, the space felt smaller, and she watched as he pulled the dripping poncho off. Beneath the rain gear, he wore a pair of camo pants and a T-shirt, and while she pretended to be absorbed in rearranging the sleeping bag on her cot, she observed him. He had set his flashlight down on the floor, and by the beam of light, she could see how his T-shirt molded itself to his contours. Charity shook herself briskly, and Chase laughed ruefully as she sprayed him with water.

"Oh, the poor thing," Kate said, and grabbed a towel from the nearby stack. Walking back toward Chase, she handed it to him. He blotted his face and then scrubbed it over his hair, before crouching down to briskly rub the dog's wet fur. Only then did she see that both his T-shirt and his pants were soaking wet.

"You're drenched," she exclaimed, returning with another towel.

"I'll dry," he said off-handedly, accepting the towel. He glanced briefly at her. "You should go back to bed."

"You won't leave?"

"I'll be right here."

Kate walked back to the bunk and climbed under the sleeping bag, curling on her side with the flashlight on the floor beside her. He stood up and was silhouetted in the beam from his own flashlight. She held her breath when he grabbed a fistful of his shirt and dragged it over his head, dropping the sodden garment onto the back of the chair.

He was breathtaking.

She released her pent-up breath on a shaky exhale. She'd realized after seeing him in the bathroom that he was fit, but the flashlight cast intriguing shadows over his body, emphasizing every dip and contour. As he toweled himself dry, she could clearly see the thrust of his shoulders and pecs. When he bent forward to blot the excess moisture from his pants, his abdomen resembled corrugated metal.

Kate felt herself growing warm. Recalling the intensity of his lovemaking the previous night, she knew he would be a good lover. Despite his size and obvious strength, his hands had been gentle on her body, coaxing a response from her until she'd been so aroused that if he hadn't pulled away when he did, she would have come just from rubbing herself against him. Even now, desire coiled tightly inside her and then unfurled, blossoming outward until her breasts ached and she shifted restlessly beneath the covers.

"You'll sleep better if you turn that light out," he offered, sitting down on the chair.

"Are you going to sit there all night?"

"That's the plan."

Kate's heart was beating fast. She reminded herself that

she didn't even know this guy, and that he'd all but told her that he had no intention of sleeping with her.

But she knew he'd lied.

There was no denying that they had chemistry. Sizzling chemistry. Maybe it was the storm that raged outside their tent, or the inherent danger that surrounded them from insurgents, but Kate had never been more desperate for human contact than she was at that moment.

Did she have the courage to proposition him? More importantly, would she have the guts to face him in the morning, regardless of whether he accepted or rejected her offer? If she did sleep with him, it would be with the knowledge that they wouldn't have any kind of relationship outside of a physical one, and even that would be short-lived. In a week, she would return home and he would resume his Ranger duties. But she also knew that she wanted this man more than she'd ever wanted any other. She'd made a lot of difficult choices in her life, some she'd regretted. This wasn't going to be one of them.

She watched as he tilted his head from side to side in an attempt to ease the tension in his neck. Charity lay on her belly beside him with her nose on her paws, and now she whined softly as Kate pushed back the covers and slid her feet to the floor. She didn't have to see Chase's face to know that his attention was riveted on her, although he never moved a muscle. His flashlight lay on the floor nearby, the beam of light angled slightly away from her, but she knew it provided sufficient light for him to see her. Outside, the wind howled and the canvas at the entrance flapped noisily.

"Kate," he warned softly.

"Shh," she whispered, standing directly in front of him. "Don't talk. I know what you're going to say, and you're wrong."

His voice was a husky rasp. "You're about to do something that you'll regret."

"Wrong again," she said, and with her heart in her throat, she slowly pulled her shirt over her head until she stood in front of him wearing only her loose flannel lounge pants and socks. She didn't try to cover herself. She wanted him to see her, to be tempted by her.

He made a sound that was half growl, half groan, and his hands formed fists on his thighs. "I'm giving you one last chance, Kate, but if you don't turn around right now and go back to bed, I won't be responsible for what happens."

But instead of retreating, Kate took a step forward, until her knees almost bumped against his. Chase's eyes glittered in the dim light as they slid over her, and his chest rose and fell swiftly, evidence that he wasn't nearly as composed as he seemed.

She didn't say anything, simply straddled his legs, forcing him to make room for her. She sat down, looping her arms around his neck. He sucked in his breath and the expression in his eyes was so heated that Kate wouldn't have been at all surprised if steam started rising from his damp skin. Her breasts brushed his chest as she leaned forward and feathered her lips over his in the barest whisper of a kiss. He groaned and turned his head, following her mouth with his own.

"Tell me that you want me," she demanded softly, and punctuated her words by taking his hand and placing it over one breast.

"Kate…" His voice was ragged.

"Tell me."

"Ah, Christ," he breathed in capitulation. He hauled her against his chest, sliding one hand over her bare back and thrusting his other hand through her hair to cup her scalp and angle her face for his kiss.

There was nothing sweet or romantic about the contact. His kiss was greedy and desperate, as if he'd hungered for her and now feared she might vanish before he could get his fill. His tongue swept past her lips and teeth to ravage the inside of her mouth. One hand slid down her back to press her closer as he ground his hips upward. He consumed her, sucking and licking at her mouth, fisting his hand in her hair to hold her still.

Kate had never experienced such complete and total possession before, and she welcomed it, sliding her arms around his shoulders and spearing her fingers through his damp hair to return his kiss eagerly. He tasted hot and sweet and his tongue slid sensuously against her own, driving her need higher. She heard a small moaning sound as she shifted closer, and realized with a sense of shock that it came from her.

"More," she managed to pant against his mouth, and cradled his head in her hands, deepening the kiss. She hardly recognized herself; she'd never been so consumed by lust, and all she could think about was the aching spot between her legs. She knew if Chase touched her there, he would find her drenched with moisture.

She gave a surprised gasp when he gripped her bottom in his hands and stood up, supporting her as if she weighed nothing. Kate locked her legs around his hips and hung on as he walked them over to the bunk and then bent forward, letting her fall back onto the mattress. As he straightened, she saw the hard thrust of his arousal beneath his camo pants, and the realization of what they were about to do hit her.

"I don't want you to stop, but what if someone comes?" she asked breathlessly, her gaze shooting toward the entrance where Charity lay and watched them curiously.

"I'm hoping that will be you," he said, his eyes glittering hotly as he looked down at her. His voice was a husky rasp. "Don't worry. You were right when you said that no-body will be out in this weather. Even if they were, they wouldn't come in."

"Are you sure?"

His hands paused in the process of unfastening his belt. "Having second thoughts?"

"No!" If he stopped now, she would die. She was sure of that. Sitting up, she brushed his hands aside and her fingers trembled as she eagerly unfastened his belt. "Definitely no second thoughts."

The buckle fell away and Kate tugged on the button of his pants until that too popped open beneath her fingers. Before she could unzip them, however, Chase sat down beside her on the narrow mattress, the metal bunk squeaking beneath their combined weight. Bending over, he unlaced his boots and pulled them off, dropping them onto the floor by the bed. Then he turned to Kate, and she felt herself tremble at the intensity of his gaze.

Chase slid a hand beneath her hair and cupped her jaw, searching her eyes in the dim light. "There's still time for you to change your mind," he said in a husky voice. "Don't get me wrong. I want you more than I've wanted anything or anyone in a very long time, but I can't make any promises to you. You'll be returning to the States in another week or so, but I'll be here for another six months."

Kate covered his hand with hers. Turning her face, she pressed a kiss into his palm. "I don't need promises," she assured him, desperately hoping he didn't hear the tremor of uncertainty in her voice. "I just want you tonight. Now."

Everything about this guy appealed to her, and it fright-ened her a little just how easily she could imagine him in her life. But she knew he was right; she couldn't keep him. She'd already decided that if she could just have him for this short time, she could walk away afterwards.

Chase gave a soft groan at her words and pushed her down on the bed, following her with the length of his body until he lay half beside and half on top of her. He braced his weight on one elbow as he slid his free hand over the curve of her rib cage and cupped one breast with a tenderness that bordered on reverence.

"I've thought of this more times in the past twenty-four hours than I can count," he admitted with a rueful laugh as he rubbed his thumb over her nipple. "Damn, you are so pretty."

Kate arched upward into his palm, and curled her legs around his hips as he dipped his head and kissed her. He fondled and caressed her breast, and the combination of his rough hand on her skin and his hot tongue in her mouth was like a drug, making her go boneless with desire.

Sliding her hands over the strong muscles of his back, she pushed at the waistband of his camo pants. He helped her to drag them down until he could kick them free of his legs, and then suddenly there he was. When he was about to bend over her again, Kate stopped him with a hand on his chest.

"Wait," she demanded, her eyes drifting over his shoulders and chest, following the deep groove that bisected his pecs and abdomen, to where his erection jutted out strongly from his body. For a moment, she couldn't breathe. "I just want to look for a minute."

"Here," he grunted, and dragged her hand down his body until she closed her fingers around his thick length. He pulsed hotly against her palm, and her heart rate quickened at the thought of having that part of him inside her. She skated her thumb over the blunt head, and it came away slick with moisture, causing an answering surge of dampness at her core. He made a guttural sound of pleasure and dropped his head to her shoulder, and Kate realized she had been stroking the length of him. His ragged breathing was a total turn-on, and she caught his mouth with hers in a deep kiss as she continued to fondle him. Overhead, the rain drummed loudly on the top of the tent, and the wind sucked at the canvas walls. But on the narrow bunk, with the warmth of the sleeping bag beneath her and Chase above her, Kate thought they might be the only two people in the world.

"Darlin'," he gasped, "you need to stop or this is going to be over before it's even started."

Reluctantly, Kate released him, but couldn't resist sliding her palms over the hard planes of his chest and torso, admiring his thick muscles. When she reached his neck, she cupped his nape and drew him down for another deep kiss. He tasted like fresh mint and smelled like spicy soap and clean, male sweat. She wanted to devour him.

"Help me take these off," she said quickly, using her free hand to push her flannel lounge pants down over her hips. Chase scooted back between her legs and hooked his thumbs in her waistband, pulling the pants off in one smooth movement. Then, with his eyes glued to her body and glittering hotly, he grasped one ankle in his hand and tugged her sock off, before doing the same to her other foot.

Kate knew she should feel embarrassed by his riveted attention, but she couldn't bring herself to feel any shame. It had been so long since anyone had looked at her as he was looking at her now; as if she were the most beautiful thing he had ever seen. Had anyone ever looked at her like that? She could no longer remember.

"Oh, man, you are so freaking gorgeous," he breathed. "But we can't do this."

FOR THE SECOND TIME in as many days, Chase had Kate Fitzgerald spread out on a bed beneath him, and while he'd believed that nothing short of a direct rocket attack would prevent him from making love to her, he'd been wrong.

Kate stared at him with a mixture of dismay and frustration. "What do you mean we can't do this?" Her voice was edged with desperation.

"Kate," he groaned, "I've been over here for six months, and I've just returned from two weeks in the field. Until yesterday, my entire focus revolved around my mission. I didn't exactly come prepared."

"Oh." Understanding dawned on her face. "Well, that's disappointing, but we could always improvise."

Chase lowered himself down beside Kate and pulled her into the curve of his body, using his free hand to leisurely explore her curves. "We could," he agreed. "In fact, we might not have another choice. As unromantic as it sounds, my job is to protect you, even in bed. I won't risk getting you pregnant."

Kate pressed against him and traced her tongue along his jaw to his ear. She caught his earlobe in her teeth and bit gently. "Then you can relax, soldier," she whispered. "I'm on the pill, and I don't have anything contagious. And I'm willing to bet that you don't, either."

Chase felt his blood begin to churn through his veins. The sensation of Kate's silken limbs entwined with his own, combined with the things she was doing with her tongue, was enough to make him discard his common sense and agree with her.

"I'm clean," he assured her.

"Well, then…" Kate rolled completely toward him and hitched one leg over his, slowly gyrating her hips against his. Her lips trailed a path along his neck and over his collarbone, while her fingers played with the small nubs of his nipples.

Flipping her onto her back, Chase used his knees to spread her thighs wide, and then caught her wrists in his hands, dragging them up over her head and pinning them there.

"I want this to last," he said, dipping his head and kissing her slowly. "But if I let you set the pace, I won't make it another five minutes. Trust me?"

She nodded, her breathing coming in fast pants. "Yes."

"Good," he smiled, "because I've been wanting to do this since I first saw you."

He kissed her slowly, a soft, moist fusing of their lips, before he moved lower, over her neck and upper chest, until he reached her breasts. He took his time, laving each one with his tongue before drawing a nipple into his mouth and sucking hard on it. Kate moaned and writhed beneath him, but Chase didn't release her. He kissed and suckled her other breast until both stood up stiff and rosy and gleaming with moisture. Then, releasing her hands, he eased backwards, dragging his mouth over her rib cage and belly, feeling her muscles contract as he moved lower.

When he reached the apex of her thighs, he skated his tongue along the seam of her thigh, and used one hand to cup her intimately. She sucked in a sharp breath and her hands flew to his wrists, which held her by the hips. Chase stilled, certain she was going to stop him. But after a moment she relaxed her grip on him. Smiling against her skin, he began to gently massage her as he kissed the inside of one thigh, and then the other.

Slowly, he slid one finger through her damp curls to the seam of her sex and gently parted her. She was slippery with arousal, and as his finger swirled over her clitoris, she gave a soft cry of pleasure and her hips jerked.

"That's it," he said approvingly.

He smoothed her curls out of the way, opening her with his fingers so that he could see the small rise of flesh that begged for attention. He glanced up the length of Kate's body and saw that she had raised her head and was watching him with eyes that were hazy with desire. Her hair was messy and spilled over her shoulders in thick waves, and her breasts rose and fell quickly with her agitated breathing. She looked like every fantasy he'd ever had, and his cock was so hard for her that he wasn't sure he'd last long enough to get inside her.

"I want to taste you," he said, his voice rough with need.

"Oh, God."

Taking that as assent, Chase bent his head and flicked his tongue over her, lightly at first, and then with increasing pressure and frequency as she moaned loudly and began rotating her hips beneath his mouth. Her fingers speared his hair, stroking and rubbing his scalp as she writhed beneath him. But when he inserted a finger into her she gasped. He could feel her inner muscles tighten around him, and knew she was close to losing control. He softened his tongue, swirling it around her clitoris as he inserted a second finger and thrust gently. Her hands gripped his head, and when he sucked on her, she cried out sharply and ground her hips against his face. He could feel her contract around his fingers, but didn't stop, drawing her orgasm out until she collapsed back against the pillow and pushed weakly at his head.

"No more," she begged. "I can't take it."

Chase withdrew, coming over her to kiss her deeply and let her taste her own essence on his lips. "Oh, you can," he assured her softly.

Reaching between their bodies, he positioned himself at her entrance and slowly surged forward, filling her. She was incredibly tight, her body closing around him so that he had a moment's certainty that he wouldn't last. Kate made a soft mewling sound, and reached down and cupped his buttocks, urging him closer.

"You feel so good," she breathed.

Oh, man, she had no idea.

He dropped his forehead to hers and paused, struggling for control.

"I want you to come again," he rasped, withdrawing and then sinking back into her in a series of thrusts that caused pressure to build at the base of his spine.

Pulling her knees back, Kate locked her ankles around his hips and wound her arms around his neck, drawing his head down for a kiss that he felt all the way to his soul. He increased his rhythm, driving himself deeper into her slick heat and feeling her inner muscles pulling at him. Kate dragged her mouth from his, her breath coming in fitful pants as she met his thrusts.

"C'mon, darlin'," he coaxed, "come for me."

Sliding a hand between their bodies, he stroked a finger over her, satisfied when he heard her sharp intake of breath and felt a renewed flood of moisture around his cock. But even as she began to tighten around him, he lost his own tenuous grip on his self-control. Overhead, a deafening crack of thunder split the air. With a hoarse shout, Chase came in a blinding rush of pleasure, aware that Kate was right there with him.

They lay together, breathing heavily for several long moments, before Chase had enough awareness to roll to his side and pull Kate into the curve of his shoulder. He pressed a kiss against her hair as the rain beat down on the canvas above their heads.

She traced a lazy pattern over his chest with one finger. "Wow," she said with a half laugh. "That was pretty amazing."

Chase had to agree. He couldn't recall the last time he'd been so turned on by a woman. Now, holding Kate in his arms, he knew that once wouldn't be enough. His rampant imagination conjured up explicit images of all the ways he wanted her, and he felt a little hollow inside at the thought of her leaving Afghanistan and returning to the States. She'd told him that she didn't need promises from him, but a part of him rebelled against having a relationship based solely on sex. For him, at least, it wasn't enough.

Gently pulling himself free, he searched for his clothing in the darkness and got dressed.

"What are you doing?" Kate asked, but her voice was heavy with sleep.

He found her shirt and helped her pull it on, and then laid her flannel pants along the bottom of the cot. She curled on her side, tucking her hands beneath the pillow.

"Try and get some sleep," he advised. "We'll be getting up early to head over to Kandahar to see the last of the concert sites."

"Aren't you going to stay the night?" Reaching out, she caught him by the belt and pulled him closer. "We have hours until morning," she murmured, but her voice was groggy and he could see she was just seconds away from slipping into total oblivion. "You don't have to leave."

Bending down, he gave her a lingering kiss, but when he pulled away, she was already asleep. "That's where you're wrong," he said softly. "If I don't leave now, then I'm totally screwed."

He pulled the sleeping bag over her shoulders and watched as she murmured incoherently and snuggled deeper into its warmth. More than anything, he wanted to slide back into the narrow bed with her and warm her with his own body heat. Chase grabbed his rain poncho and pulled it on. He paused only briefly at the entrance to the tent before he ducked his head and ventured outside, acknowledging that he'd lied to Kate.

He was already screwed.

10

IF IT WEREN'T FOR the deliciously tender places on her body, Kate might have imagined Chase's heated lovemaking of the previous night. He had awakened her the following morning by calling her name through the entrance of the tent, but he hadn't come in, telling her she had thirty minutes to get dressed and meet him outside.

The storm had passed during the night, and the morning air was clear. Even at that hour, the sun beat relentlessly down, drying the muddy roads and promising a hot afternoon. Kate packed her bags and went outside to meet Chase. He stood leaning against a Humvee reading his handheld device, while Charity lay at his feet, her tongue lolling. She called his name, feeling inexplicably shy. He looked up and for just an instant she saw the same heat in his eyes that she had seen last night. His gaze raked over her once, before he schooled his expression into one of cool politeness.

"Good morning," he said, pushing away from the vehicle to walk toward her. "Did you sleep well?"

She gave him a meaningful smile. "Like a baby. But what about you? You didn't need to leave."

He paused beside her. "Yeah," he said quietly. "I did.

What happened last night was amazing, Kate, but it can't happen again."

Kate's smile faltered and something twisted painfully in her chest. "You're saying it was a mistake."

Chase's expression was so intense that for a moment Kate thought he was going to pull her into his arms. "No," he said fiercely. "Not a mistake. Just not very smart, considering our situation."

Realistically, she knew he was right. Last night, she'd been convinced that she could have sex with Chase and not have any regrets; that she could have a brief fling without getting emotionally involved. But recalling what it had been like…what *he* had been like, she knew she'd been kidding herself.

Now she forced herself to nod in agreement. "I understand."

A muscle ticked in his jaw and he took a step toward her. For an instant, she thought he might actually kiss her. Instead, he made a small sound of frustration and ducked into her tent, reappearing a moment later with one of her duffel bags in either hand.

"You can use this protective gear for the remainder of your visit," he said gruffly, indicating the bag that contained her flak vest and helmet.

Kate watched as he walked quickly to the Humvee and tossed the equipment into the backseat. She wanted to tell him that he could take the stuff. There wasn't enough protective gear in the world to keep her heart safe from him.

Drawing a deep breath, Kate walked slowly to the Humvee and climbed into the passenger seat, placing her shoulder bag on the floor at her feet. She reminded herself that she was thirty-one years old and she had wanted Chase in her bed. In fact, he'd given her several opportunities to back off, but she'd been determined to have him. He'd been upfront with her about not being able to make any commitments. It wasn't as though he'd misled her. She had no reason to expect that he would suddenly treat her as if they were soul mates.

So why did she feel so miserable?

She watched as he opened the back of the Humvee and let the dog jump in before he climbed into the driver's seat and thrust the vehicle into gear. The roads were thick with mud and washed-out in some places, but the Humvee bounced over the ruts without any problem.

"Here," he said, handing her a paper bag. "I brought you some breakfast. And a coffee."

Kate accepted the bag, expecting to find another Pop-Tart pastry. Instead, she found a hot breakfast sandwich and some fruit inside. The unexpected gesture both touched and confused her.

"Thank you. Did you already eat?"

"What? Oh, yeah. I didn't get any sleep last night after we—" He broke off abruptly. "I was at the dining facility around 4:00 a.m." He glanced at her as he spoke, and twin patches of color rode high on his cheekbones, the only indication that he was thinking about their interlude, and that he wasn't as unfeeling about it as he would have her believe. Suddenly, Kate felt much lighter.

"Oh, well, thanks." She took a bite of the sandwich, realizing for the first time how hungry she was. Then she recalled the helicopter flight from Bagram to Camp Leatherneck, and felt her stomach rebel. "How are we getting to Kandahar?"

A brief smile touched his mouth, but he didn't look at her. "Not by Black Hawk."

"Perfect."

They headed back to the flight line, and Kate looked

across the tarmac to one of the biggest aircraft she had ever seen. Stuffing her sandwich in the bag, she turned to Chase.

"That's a C-17 Globemaster," he said, nodding toward the plane. "One of the Marine expeditionary units is transferring to Kandahar and bringing three Humvees with them, but they have some extra seats, so we're hitching a ride with them."

Kate swallowed hard, reminding herself that at least it wasn't a Black Hawk, and at least they didn't have to drive overland.

Inside the makeshift terminal, Chase took her body armor out of her duffel bag and handed it to her, and then pulled on his own protective gear. Outside, he snapped a long lead to Charity's harness and handed the end to Kate, who watched as he threw their duffel bags on a pallet, alongside dozens of other bags and assorted gear. Several soldiers began rearranging the baggage and then strapped it all down with an enormous net.

A military bus drew to a stop by the pallets. "This is our ride to the plane," Chase said, taking the leash and indicating she should precede him.

"Sir, I'm sorry but the dog isn't allowed on the flight," said a military police officer, stepping forward to prevent Chase from boarding.

Kate thought Chase might try to argue with the man, but instead he pulled a small card out of his pocket and showed it to the officer, who saluted smartly and stepped back. "My mistake, sir. Enjoy your flight."

They managed to get two seats together near the front of the bus, and Charity scooted in under their feet. Kate turned to Chase.

"What was that you showed the soldier?" she asked.

Reaching into his pocket, Chase withdrew an official looking ID card, but this one had a photo of Charity, and beneath it the words *Military Working Dog,* and what Kate guessed was the number of Chase's unit.

"Is she really a working dog?" she asked in surprise. "I thought she was a stray that you rescued."

"She is a stray, but the K-9 unit has been working with her for the past six months." Chase reached down to rub the dog's ears. "Her test scores are higher than most of the other dogs, and her conditioning is exceptional. My guess is that she was a military working dog with the Afghan army and somehow got separated from her handler and ended up in that village. She's not actually part of the K-9 team, but the unit was good enough to give her an ID card so that I can bring her with me when I travel."

"What about when you return to the States?" Kate asked. "Will you be able to take her home with you?"

He shrugged, but Kate didn't miss the regret in his eyes. "Probably not. Officially, she's not on any military roster and there are strict prohibitions about adopting local dogs. I'm fortunate that nobody has objected to my rescuing her, but locally adopted pets aren't allowed to travel in crates owned by the military, nor are they permitted to fly on military flights back to the States."

Kate stared at him. "You're not going to leave her here?"

"I don't want to, but the logistics of transporting her to a commercial airport and getting her on board are complicated. I can't accompany her myself so I'll need to find a sponsor to travel with her and make the right connections. That's difficult and expensive."

They fell silent, and Kate considered what would happen to Charity if she were left in Afghanistan. The K-9 unit might continue to look out for her after Chase left, but eventually they would return to the States, too. What would happen to the dog then?

She watched as dozens of soldiers climbed on board and

shuffled past them, all wearing helmets and flak vests and carrying heavy backpacks. She drew curious glances from most of them, but one look at Chase's face and they moved quickly past. When the bus was filled, it rumbled away from the terminal and across the tarmac, and pulled up alongside the enormous plane. Chase stood up, blocking the aisle so that Kate could slip out in front of him and exit the bus. On the tarmac, she gaped. There was no set of stairs. Instead, the entire back of the aircraft was open and a wide ramp extended onto the runway.

Kate watched as soldiers climbed up the ramp and disappeared into the cavernous interior. She looked questioningly at Chase.

"This way," he said, and with the dog in the lead, he took her elbow to help her up the ramp. At the top, Kate couldn't suppress a gasp.

"Are those Humvees?" she asked in astonishment.

Three of the military vehicles were parked end to end down the center of the plane, secured to the floor with chains and enormous nets. Along the walls were dozens of jump seats, and Kate watched as the soldiers quickly sat down with their backpacks on their knees.

"Sit here," Chase said, and drew Kate down onto a canvas seat with nylon webbing for the back. Chase took the one next to her, and after ensuring that her seatbelt was fastened, tucked her shoulder bag beneath his feet and gave Charity a command to lie down. "Comfortable?"

Kate couldn't imagine anything more uncomfortable, but understood that this was a military flight, designed for efficiency, not comfort. "It's fine," she assured him.

Within fifteen minutes, the rear of the aircraft closed and it began taxiing down the runway. There were no windows in the plane, and the interior was simply an enormous cavern of wiring, buttons and electrical equipment. The three

Humvees were so close that if she stretched out her legs, her feet would touch the wheels, and it was impossible to see anything in the rest of the plane because their sheer size blocked her view. With a sigh, she put her head back and closed her eyes. But she was acutely conscious of the man who sat so close beside her that she could feel his pant leg brush against her own, hear his breathing, and smell the unique scent that she had come to associate with him.

"We'll be at Kandahar in about ninety minutes," Chase said, as the big plane lifted into the air.

She nodded. The roar of the engines effectively prevented any conversation, so she simply closed her eyes again. The throb of the engines lulled her into a state of relaxation, and she passed the time by recalling the events of the previous night in minute detail. It seemed no time had passed, when suddenly the big plane banked steeply and began to descend.

Kate glanced beside her, but Chase had his head tipped back against the seat and his eyes closed. Even in sleep, he was mouthwatering, and she allowed herself the luxury of studying his features. The soldiers closest to her were alert, but not alarmed, so she wasn't worried. The plane continued to bank and descend, though, as if it were riding an invisible roller-coaster track.

"Why is it doing that?" she asked Chase. "It feels like we're spiraling downward."

"We are actually," he said. "The pilot is making what's called a combat landing, descending in a tight spiral to make us less vulnerable to attack."

At the last minute, the plane leveled out and the wheels bounced against the runway. They had landed, and Kate watched as the soldiers began gathering their gear. Tenley and her band would arrive here in just two days, and Kate would be fully occupied with ensuring her sister had everything she needed. Suddenly, Kate wasn't ready for Tenley to intrude. She wasn't ready to slip back into her role of provider, counselor and surrogate parent to her sister. Most importantly, she wasn't ready to give up Chase. She wasn't naive enough to think that once Tenley arrived, she would have any time with him. She knew his focus would shift from escorting her to protecting the entire group of performers. She would have no more opportunity to be alone with him.

Less than a week ago, she never would have thought she'd meet someone in Afghanistan who aroused her enough to sleep with him, knowing that the likelihood of having any kind of meaningful relationship was next to nil. She'd had one-night stands and brief flings before, and they always left her feeling empty and lonely. She'd decided a long time ago that she wouldn't do that to herself again. She deserved better. She wanted the whole package, including the house, the white picket fence and the happy-ever-after. But she also knew that she'd never meet a man like Chase again, and even if she'd never have a repeat of their night together, she had no regrets.

The plane taxied to the terminal, and the rear ramp lowered. With Charity's lead in one hand, Chase carried Kate's bag over his shoulder and took her elbow as they disembarked and waited while the pallets of baggage were removed and placed along the flight line.

Fifteen minutes later, they were in the backseat of another Humvee, with two soldiers up front. Chase helped Kate remove her protective gear and stowed it away in the duffel bag, before removing his own.

"We won't need to wear this unless the sirens go off," he said. "Let's get you settled and go get something to eat, and then I'll bring you over to the concert site. This is an enormous base, and you'll have semi-private housing here."

"How many troops are here?" Kate asked, but just looking out the window of the Humvee told her that this was no forward operating base.

"There are more than twenty thousand coalition troops stationed here, and hundreds of civilian contractors." He slanted her an amused look. "There's even a boardwalk with some American fast-food restaurants and a bazaar of sorts where vendors sell local goods. We could walk over there and grab a bite."

Looking out the window, she noticed that the air was hazy and had a yellowish tinge to it.

"Is this smog of some kind?" she asked, having seen something similar in California.

"No, ma'am," replied the driver. "What you're seeing is dust. The air is always full of it, even indoors."

They drove in silence for several more minutes, and Kate was astonished at the sheer size of the base. "I expect the USO brings a lot of entertainers here, given how big the place is," she commented.

"I expect so," said Chase. "You're the first celebrity assignment I've had, and I spend so much time in the field or at the remote operating bases that I don't usually catch any performances. At any rate, the local USO is accustomed to providing accommodations for visiting celebrities and dignitaries, so I think you'll find the conditions here are much better than at Bagram or Camp Leatherneck."

In other words, there was no chance that she would end up alone in a tent where she would need to rely on Chase to watch over her. Even if she did, there was little likelihood that she would get a repeat performance of the previous night.

Leaning forward, Chase spoke quietly to the driver, directing him. Kate was amazed at the number of soldiers, military vehicles and buildings that they passed. They had been driving for fifteen minutes and still had not reached their destination. The Humvee pulled up in front of a long row of modified trailers, each reinforced with sandbags. They were housing units, Kate realized, nearly identical to Chase's CHU back on Bagram.

"Is this it?" she asked, as Chase pulled her luggage out of the back and commanded Charity to stay.

"This is where you'll be housed with Tenley," Chase confirmed. "This entire row is reserved by the USO. They don't have any empty units at the moment, but there are two female actors in one of the trailers, and they have an extra bunk bed that the USO said you and your sister can use."

"That's great," Kate said, meaning it. She had no desire to sleep in a tent by herself, especially now that Chase wouldn't be spending the night with her. "Do you know who the women are?"

Chase shrugged. "I don't, sorry."

Inside the unit, Chase dropped her bags on the floor by the nearest set of bunk beds. Kate looked around curiously. There was one large bedroom in the front, with a bunk bed against either wall and a sofa under the front window. The two bottom bunks were obviously occupied, with overnight bags sitting on top of the blankets, and a pair of shoes under each bed. The interior of the unit was unpainted plywood, and someone had tried to make the place more cheerful by hanging posters on the wall.

Kate turned to Chase. "How long will the other two women be here?"

Chase leaned against the open door frame. "They're leaving tomorrow on the return flight that your sister and the other performers are arriving on. Why? Would it be a problem if they were staying?"

"No," she assured him. "This will work out beautifully. Where will you be?"

He paused, halfway to the door. "In a barracks hut. You have my beeper. I'll be close by."

Kate chewed her bottom lip, understanding that there would be no opportunity for them to be together tonight. Still, she couldn't just let him walk away, at least not without trying to convince him that last night meant something to her, and that if he was willing, they could have some kind of relationship. She knew that Chase would be here in Afghanistan for another six months, but that didn't matter to her. She'd been alone for a long time. Waiting six months for someone like Chase would be no hardship—if he agreed.

"Chase," she called softly, before he could leave. "Wait."

He turned in the doorway, and for an instant she saw an expression in his eyes—a combination of agony and hope—that gave her courage. "What is it?" he asked, glancing toward the Humvee, where the two soldiers sat waiting for them.

"Chase...about last night...I know you think it was a mistake, but you're wrong."

Something twisted in his face as he looked back at her. "Kate. Last night was...well, it was incredible. Would I like a repeat performance? Damned straight." He muttered a curse beneath his breath and raked a hand over his hair. "But Jesus, Kate, there's no future in it, and I can't—I can't—" He broke off and turned to stare out the door toward the street, where vehicles drove past and several soldiers walked by.

Kate stared at his rigid back, and then took a step toward him, but didn't dare touch him. "What?" she asked softly. "What can't you do, Chase?"

He turned around and Kate took an involuntary step backwards at the expression on his face. "I can't be around you without wanting you. It took all my strength to leave you last night, but it can't happen again, Kate. It's not fair to you. Or to me."

"Chase, I know you didn't want to escort me around, and that you have more important issues on your mind—" He started to interrupt and she held up a hand to forestall him. "But last night meant something to me. And I think it meant something to you, too."

Chase made a growling sound of frustration. "It doesn't matter if it meant something to me or not. Tomorrow your focus will shift to your sister, which is great. That's your job. But five days later, you'll be gone."

Kate took a step toward him. "Then we shouldn't waste any time."

Reaching out, she put a hand along the side of his jaw and reached up to press a lingering kiss against his mouth. He resisted for several seconds, and then with a groan, his arms came around her, and he lowered his head, covering her mouth with his own. Kicking the door shut, he walked her backward until the backs of her knees bumped against the sofa and she sat down. He followed, pushing her against the cushions, his lips still fused to hers.

Kate welcomed him, winding her arms around his neck and pulling him down on top of her. He kissed her deeply, spearing his hands into her hair.

"God, you taste good," he muttered against her lips. "I still think this is a bad idea, but I have no willpower where you're concerned."

Kate smiled against his face. "And here I was beginning to think that you might not like me."

Chase groaned, and planting another kiss on her mouth, pulled her with him to a sitting position. "My problem has nothing to do with not liking you, and everything to do with liking you too much," he growled.

"Then find a way for us to be together tonight," she

breathed, searching his eyes. "If this is the last night we have alone before I go home, spend it with me. This base is huge. There must be somewhere we can go to be alone. You know you want to."

He gave her a tolerant look and stood up, rubbing a hand across the back of his neck. "Jesus, Kate, it has nothing to do with what I want or don't want to do. Last night was different. We were in the middle of a monsoon and there was no chance that anyone was going to catch us together in that tent. But things are different here. Neither of us has our own unit, and even if there was a place that we could go, you can be sure that someone else will already have found it."

Kate nodded. "Okay. I would never want to get you in trouble. I just want to spend time with you before I leave."

"I want that, too, believe me." He glanced out the window at the waiting Humvee. "But if we don't make an appearance within the next minute, those soldiers are going to start getting ideas about what we're doing in here. In fact, I'm pretty sure they saw you kiss me before I shut the door."

"Oh." Kate glanced toward the closed door. "Then we should definitely get outside before your reputation is completely ruined."

Chase gave a rueful laugh. "Too late, darlin'. I think my reputation was destroyed the moment I laid eyes on you. I haven't been able to focus on anything but you since I first saw you standing in the terminal at Bagram."

"Well, considering I'm your current assignment, you *should* be focused on me."

"Yeah, well, let's get back to the vehicle before I become so focused on you that I forget everything else." He opened the door and placed a hand at the small of her back, indicating she should precede him.

As she climbed into the backseat, Kate didn't miss the knowing look the two soldiers gave each other before they stoically fixed their attention straight ahead. But as Chase climbed in beside her, he covered her hand with his own and squeezed her fingers, letting her know that even though he might be on duty, he no longer considered her to be his duty.

11

AFTER A LONG day of visiting the concert sites, meeting with the USO representatives, and exploring the small bazaar at the center of the base, Kate returned to her housing unit after dinner to find it occupied by her two roommates. Both women were in their forties, and welcomed Kate with a mug of hot tea brewed in an electric kettle that sat on the small side table. The women played characters on a popular sitcom. Kate knew she should recognize them, but she rarely watched television, preferring movies or books when she had any spare time.

"So, what brings a pretty young thing like you out here all by yourself?" asked Jessica Cochran.

"You have to ask?" Marion O'Connell gave a suggestive wink. "Have you looked around here? There are literally hundreds of good-looking, hard-bodied young men running around. I'll tell you what. If I was as young and attractive as Kate, I'd be looking for excuses to come over here on a regular basis!"

Kate laughed. "Well, I agree that some of the guys are pretty amazing, but I'm hoping this will be my first and last visit."

"The USO said you're a singer?" asked Jessica, sipping her tea.

"Not me," Kate said quickly. "I'm Tenley Miles's publicist. I came over a few days early just to check things out and make sure everything's ready for her. She flies in tomorrow."

"Tenley Miles?" Marion's face lit up with recognition. "My niece adores her. But wasn't she involved in some recent scandal?"

Kate took a gulp of hot tea, hoping to avoid answering, but Marion was going through her mental Rolodex of celebrity scandals until finally her expression registered recognition.

"I know," Marion declared in triumph. "She made some disparaging remarks about the military. I'm surprised she wants to come over here and entertain the troops, considering some of the negative things she had to say."

"Yes, well that's why we decided to come," Kate admitted. "Tenley's only eighteen and she can be impulsive. She doesn't really mean what she said, and we're hoping that this tour will help to demonstrate that."

Jessica shook her head and made a tsking sound. "I don't know. You can do a lot of stupid stuff, but when you start maligning our men and women in uniform, that can be a tough one to recover from."

Kate set her cup down. "I think I'll head over into the shower before it gets too late."

"That's a great idea," Marion said, putting her own teacup aside. "I hate the thought of walking all that way by myself."

"How far is it?" Kate asked. She had been looking forward to calling Chase on his beeper so that he could walk with her.

"It's about a ten minute hike," Jessica replied, gathering her gear together.

Realizing she had no valid reason to call Chase, Kate

reluctantly pulled her toiletries out of her duffel bag, along with a clean change of clothes. It was still light outside as they set off. At the end of the road, they turned left and continued along another row of housing units, until Kate saw the shower facilities in the distance. They passed groups of soldiers, who nodded politely to them, and twice they had to stop so that Marion and Jessica could sign autographs.

While Kate waited for them, she noticed a female soldier walk past and found herself staring, mainly because she was so tall. Kate guessed the woman was close to six feet, but she walked with a feminine, athletic grace. Rather than the typical camouflage uniform, she wore a green flight suit, and something about her struck Kate as familiar. As the woman drew closer, she looked at Kate and smiled.

Kate raised a hand in greeting, recognizing the woman as the Black Hawk pilot who had flown both her and Chase from Bagram Air Base to Camp Leatherneck. She watched as Captain Larson stopped outside one of the housing units and fitted a key into the door, opening it and disappearing inside. Kate frowned, wondering if Chase knew that she was at Kandahar. She recalled the way the other woman had looked at Chase when they had boarded the helicopter, making her suspect they might be involved. She couldn't blame the other woman for ogling Chase; he was pretty hot. But she knew she wouldn't be the one telling him that Captain Larson was less than a stone's throw away.

"Are you okay, hon?"

Jessica was watching Kate with a mixture of concern and curiosity.

"I'm fine," she assured the older woman. "I thought I saw someone I knew, but I was wrong."

"Well let's get going. I want to be back in our own little house before it gets dark."

Jessica was right; daylight was disappearing, and the temperatures was dropping. But the showers were private and hot, and Kate took her time under the steaming spray until she could hear the other women in the outer changing area.

Kate quickly dried herself off and got dressed, wrapping a towel around her wet hair for the walk back. When they left the shower facilities, the sun had set and the sky was beginning to darken. Kate listened to Marion and Jessica's chatter, mostly gossip about the sitcom and who they thought would get the ax next.

As they turned the corner to the street where Captain Larson's housing unit was located, Kate saw a familiar figure walking toward them. *Chase.* Her pulse kicked into overdrive in anticipation and her hand flew self-consciously to the towel wrapped around her head. He was still more than fifty feet away, and hadn't yet seen her and her companions rounding the corner.

She couldn't prevent a smile, and was about to call his name when he suddenly stopped and knocked lightly on Captain Larson's door. Kate stopped, too, stunned when the pilot opened for him. Unaware that they had an audience, Captain Larson reached up and planted a lingering kiss on Chase's mouth, before she drew him inside and closed the door quickly behind him. Although the shade in the small window was pulled down, Kate saw a shadow pass in front of it, and then another. But when the two shadows merged, there was no doubt in her mind what was happening behind that closed door, and for a moment she thought she might actually be ill.

She continued walking, her eyes glued to the silhouette of the embracing couple. As she drew alongside the unit, Kate heard the distinct sound of a man's voice, followed by Captain Larson's low, throaty laugh.

Both Jessica and Marion gave each other knowing looks, and Kate hoped the fading light disguised her own stricken expression. It took all her strength not to race up to the door and wrench it open.

Instead, she tipped her chin up, aware that her breathing was coming in quick, shallow pants. Her throat felt tight and her chest ached. What had he said to her just hours earlier? That he had no willpower where she was concerned? It seemed he had no willpower where Captain Larson was concerned, either. She recalled his agonized words as he'd turned away from her in the housing unit. *There's no future in it, and I can't—I can't—*

It all made sense to Kate now.

The reason there was no future in it was because he was already committed—to Captain Larson. She nearly groaned aloud. He'd tried to tell her that they had no chance for a relationship, and she hadn't listened. But he hadn't put up much resistance, and he certainly hadn't seemed overly concerned about his pilot girlfriend when he'd spent the night with Kate in her tent.

She was such an idiot. When would she ever learn?

They reached their housing unit, and Kate made a pretense of being interested in the women's conversation until she thought she might scream.

"You know, I have a splitting headache," she fibbed. "Would you mind if I just climbed into my bunk and went to bed?"

"Oh, honey," Marion said in sympathy, "you go right ahead. In fact, we'll go to bed, too, and then the light won't disturb you."

"Oh, no," Kate protested. "Please don't do that on my account. Besides, I overheard you telling Jessica how much you were looking forward to another cup of tea, so you should have one. I promise you, I'm so tired that nothing will disturb me."

After convincing the two women to have their tea, Kate

climbed up into the top bunk and pulled the blankets over her shoulders, turning her face toward the wall. She replayed the scene over and over again in her mind. At one point, she'd nearly convinced herself that it wasn't Chase she'd seen; it had been another soldier who'd merely resembled him. But when Captain Larson had opened the door, the interior light had clearly revealed his face. There was no doubt in her mind that it had been Chase. She still couldn't believe how well he'd hidden his feelings for the pilot when they'd flown in her helicopter. Captain Larson hadn't hidden her interest in Chase, but he had been all business.

Kate lay curled on her side and determined that he would never know how much he'd hurt her. If he'd been honest with her and had just told her that he was already involved with someone else, she would have backed off. But he hadn't. He'd taken full advantage of everything she'd offered. She'd been foolish enough to sleep with him, but it wouldn't happen again. She deserved better. Tomorrow, she thought fiercely, things would change. She would be all business, and nothing Chase said or did would break through the protective barrier she was erecting around her heart.

CHASE SPENT THE NIGHT at the Special Ops headquarters office on base. He and the special-operations teams stationed at Kandahar performed many joint missions, and one of them was the hunt and capture of Al-Azir. The previously issued stand-down order was still in effect, but that didn't prevent him and his team of commandos from gathering intelligence and planning their next move. Chase and the other team members spent hours analyzing satellite photos and images taken from their drone aircraft, which indicated a large group of men had left the village where Al-Azir had been hiding, and had moved into the nearby mountains.

Chase knew the area was riddled with caves, and that

Al Azir and his men could successfully hide out there for months. But at least they had an idea where he had fled to, and once the stand-down order was lifted, his team would resume their hunt for him.

Having gotten less than four hours of sleep on a cot in the back room of the operations shack, Chase woke up at dawn and made his way to the showers. He passed the housing unit where Kate was staying, and his footsteps slowed. Had she been in there alone, nothing would have prevented him from going inside and climbing into her bunk with her. He desperately wanted to be with her again, and he'd known a keen sense of frustration when the USO personnel had told him that she would not have her own housing unit while at Kandahar. With her sister arriving that morning, there would be no opportunity for them to be alone again before she returned to the States. Reluctantly, he continued past Kate's unit toward the showers. He was lost in his own thoughts and didn't see the soldier who stepped quietly out of a housing unit on his left, until he heard his name called.

"Chase!"

He stopped and turned, surprised to see his brother walking swiftly toward him. "Hey, I was wondering if I might see you here," he said, grabbing his brother's hand and pulling him into a swift, hard hug. "I thought you might be up at Kabul."

They drew apart, and Chase stared at his brother's face, identical to his own except for the perpetual cocky grin.

"I was," Chance grinned, "but they sent us down here yesterday to provide cover for a VIP visit."

Major Chance Rawlins was an Apache helicopter pilot, permanently stationed at Bagram Air Base, although his missions frequently took him to the other bases in Afghanistan. He and Captain Jenna Larson had had a brief fling several months earlier, when they'd both been assigned to

Fort Bragg in North Carolina. But when she'd turned up in Afghanistan, Chance had been quick to turn their relationship into something a little more permanent. Now the two were committed to each other.

Chase glanced from his brother to the housing unit he had just left, and felt a smile tug at his mouth. "I take it you didn't stay alone last night?"

Chance's eyes gleamed. "Are you kidding? How often are Jenna and I ever on the same base? Just try keeping me away from her."

"Yeah, well, don't get caught."

His brother sobered. "She's returning to the States in just a few weeks, while I'll be over here for another six months. Man, that's going to suck."

Chase felt his brother's pain, he really did. Just the thought of Kate leaving made his chest feel tight. He hadn't really explored his feelings for Kate, but he knew he wasn't ready to say goodbye to her. Not by a long shot.

"How long are you going to be at Kandahar?" he asked.

Chance shrugged. "I'm scheduled to escort a VIP to Bagram tomorrow, but Jenna left around 4:00 a.m. this morning for the Kalagush region."

Captain Larson's primary mission was to transport troops and personnel from one base to another, and although she was assigned to Kandahar, her missions took her to every base in Afghanistan, including some of the remote operating bases. She usually flew in tandem with another Black Hawk, and sometimes with an Apache escort, as well.

"So I take it you're not flying escort with her?"

Chance shook his head. "No such luck, I'm afraid." Reaching out, he gave Chase's shoulder a friendly punch. "But what the hell are you doing here? Jenna said she gave you a lift from Bagram to Camp Leatherneck, but I didn't know you were going to be here at Kandahar." His grin widened. "Not that I would have changed my plans with her to come and see you, of course. So why are you here?"

"The Pentagon has temporarily halted all special-operations missions," Chase said grimly.

"Ah," Chance replied. "I heard an airstrike went wrong about thirty miles from here last week. Is that why you're here? Part of the investigation?"

Chase gave a snort. "Hardly. I was yanked out of the field and given a personal security assignment."

"Really?" His brother's face registered interest. "Anyone good?"

Oh, yeah.

Chase shrugged. "Some teenaged country singer and her publicist. Part of the big Independence Day concert tour that begins tonight."

"Oh, man. I'm sorry, bro. I know how you hate those assignments."

"Yeah." His voice was noncommittal. He hated the assignment so much that he couldn't wait to get showered and dressed and over to Kate's housing unit to see her. But he wouldn't tell his brother just how soft he'd become. Chance would have a field day if he knew his tough-as-nails, all-business brother had violated even one rule for the sake of a woman.

To his surprise, Chance burst out laughing.

"What?" he demanded.

"Man, you are so freaking transparent," Chance said, still laughing. "Jenna told me all about your *assignment*. A pretty, curvy brunette who looked like she wanted to kill Jenna for just talking with you." He gave Chase a knowing look. "You dog. You put the moves on her, didn't you? C'mon, you can fool some people with your badass attitude, but not me, bro. I can see the truth. It's written all over your face. You *like* this woman."

He said it as a statement of fact, and not a question. But he was right; Chase had never been able to keep a secret from his twin and there was no point in even trying.

He blew out a hard breath. "Jesus, Chance, I've been with her all of three days and she's so deep under my skin…" He scrubbed a hand over his hair. "But her client, the singer, flies in today, so it's not like we're going to have any chance to be alone again. And then in five more days, she leaves."

Chance considered him for a long moment. "Okay, I tell you what. Jenna already left. She'll be gone for at least a week. I was going to crash in her unit tonight, but I can always go bunk with the itinerant pilots. Why don't you and your lady friend use her place tonight? Hell, use it for as long as you're going to be here. I know Jenna won't mind."

The offer was so tempting that Chase was half inclined to retrieve Kate right then and drag her over to Captain Larson's housing unit just so he could be alone with her. He ached to feel her body pressed against his own, and needed to hear her small cries of pleasure as he made love to her. He couldn't remember the last time he'd been so eager to spend time with a woman.

Now he shook his brother's hand. "Thanks. I appreciate the offer."

"You bet. Look, I have to run, but it was great to see you."

"You, too," Chase said, and gave Chance the key to Captain Larson's unit. "You take care of yourself, okay?"

He watched as Chance jogged away, then continued walking to the showers feeling lighter and more hopeful. He would be with Kate again that night, even if it was just for a few hours. He'd find someone to keep an eye on Kate's sister for the time that they would be away from her.

Whistling softly under his breath, he thought the coming day might just be the best one he'd spent in Afghanistan so far.

12

PULLING ON HER SHOES, Kate decided this was going to be the worst day of her life. Even the prospect of seeing Tenley again didn't raise her spirits. If anything, she felt exhausted at the idea of looking after her sister for the next several days. She just wanted the tour to be over and to return to the States. She'd spent most of the night lying in her bed thinking about her own future. One that didn't include Major Chase Rawlins. Just the thought of him brought a painful lump to her chest.

Once the tour was over, she would return to Nashville with Tenley, but she'd decided that it was time to find her own place to live. She would continue to act as Tenley's publicist, since it was clear that her sister needed her, but there was no reason for them to continue to live together. And then perhaps, in a couple of years, she could persuade Tenley to find another publicist. As for Chase...she would chalk it up as a learning experience and not make the same mistake again.

She gave her laces a hard yank. Did Captain Larson have any idea that Chase wasn't faithful to her? Maybe they had an open relationship. Kate didn't know and didn't care; she only knew that she could never share Chase with another woman. She had a vivid image of him making love to the pilot, and her stomach twisted.

"You okay, hon?"

Kate jerked her head up to see Jessica standing in the open door of the housing unit, watching her closely. She nodded and finished tying her other shoe. "Never better. My client comes in today and we can finally get this show on the road. I'm just anxious to get this over with so I can go home."

"Amen," Jessica said, leaving the door open as she came in. "We missed you at breakfast this morning, but I brought you a nice pastry." She held out the offering, neatly folded in a white napkin. "Full of lemon custard. Looks delicious."

Kate forced a smile and sat up straight on the small sofa. "Thank you, that was very thoughtful."

"Oh, no bother at all," Jessica replied, sitting down on the lower bunk, across from Kate. "So how are you really doing? You look a little peaked to me."

Kate waved a dismissive hand. "No, I'm fine, really. Like I said, I'm just looking forward to going home." She turned to pick up her watch from the side table. "I've decided that as much as I respect and admire what the troops are doing over here, if I never see another uniform in my life, it will be too soon. *You* might think they're all hotties, but from what I can tell of the ones I've met, they're just walking testosterone in combat boots."

The masculine clearing of a throat had her turning guiltily toward the door, where Chase's broad shoulders nearly blocked the daylight. He looked so strong and commanding in his uniform and his sunglasses that for a moment Kate's heart leaped. Then the scene from the previous night came rushing back, and she determinedly looked away.

"Hmm," murmured Jessica with a knowing smile. "You were saying?"

Kate stood up, but didn't apologize, despite the fact she knew that Chase had overheard her disparaging remarks.

"Good morning," she said, picking up her shoulder bag.

The sunlight behind him cast his face in shadow, and with his sunglasses on, it was impossible to read his expression. "Good morning," he said carefully. "If you're ready, we can head over to the concert site and check it out. Your client's flight isn't due to arrive for another two hours, which leaves us plenty of time."

"Fine," she said coolly. She turned to Jessica and Marion. "It was really nice meeting both of you. Maybe I'll see you over at the flight line, but in case I don't, have a safe trip back to the States."

Marion gave her a hug. "Just remember that most guys are jerks," she whispered in Kate's ear. "Don't be too hard on him."

Kate gave her a stiff smile and pulled away.

"Now you listen to me," Jessica whispered, as she hugged Kate. "I don't know who this guy is, but I do know that he isn't deserving of a second look from you. I saw what he was up to last night, too, so don't you give him the time of day."

Pulling away, Kate smiled at both women and turned to Chase. He jerked his sunglasses off and frowned, his sharp gaze sweeping her from head to toe and missing nothing.

"Everything okay?" he asked as they walked toward the Humvee that waited for them. "You have shadows under your eyes. Didn't you sleep?"

"Not really," she said stiffly. "Looks like you didn't get much sleep, either."

"I managed to grab a couple of hours."

Kate barely suppressed a disdainful snort. She didn't want to think about what Chase had been doing that prevented him from sleeping, and she certainly didn't want him to know that she had witnessed him kissing Captain Larson.

He was the Special Ops guy; let him figure out why she was in a bitchy mood this morning.

They rode in silence for several long minutes. She could sense his puzzlement and his concern, but refused to look over at him, or speak.

"Are you sure everything is okay?" he finally asked. "Because if there's anything you need to talk about, I'm here for you." His voice was so warm and compassionate that Kate's resolve almost wavered.

Almost.

Instead, she turned and gave Chase a level look, despite the fact her heart was hammering inside her chest. "I'm fine. Really."

"You know," he mused, "I grew up on a ranch in Texas, and while it was just my parents and me and my brother, my uncle owned the neighboring ranch. He had five daughters. *Five.* Those girls spent as much time on our ranch as they did on their own, and I became pretty good at interpreting their moods."

Kate gave him a tolerant look. "So?"

"So I know that when a woman says things like 'I'm fine,' and 'Really,' what she's actually saying is 'Screw you, I'm pissed at you,' and 'Leave me alone.'"

Kate couldn't prevent her quick smile, but then she sobered. "Well then, if you've broken the code, you should heed the hidden message."

"What's going on, Kate? You can tell me anything."

Kate gave a disdainful laugh and turned her attention out the window. "Thanks, but I don't think so. Why don't we just go look at the site, okay?"

She sensed his frustration, but he was nothing if not intuitive, and thankfully he didn't pursue the topic. They drove in silence after that, until they arrived at an enormous parade field with a covered stage at the far end. Both the field and the stage swarmed with soldiers and technicians who were busy running electrical cables and wires, and setting up the amplifiers and speakers. A gigantic American flag provided the backdrop for the performers, and Kate watched as the lighting specialists flicked through all of the possible combinations.

"Wow," she said, climbing out of the Humvee.

She walked toward the stage, taking note of the work being performed all around her. Along the perimeter of the parade field, food tents had been set up and Kate watched as the soldiers dragged out long tables and prepared enormous grills for what would surely be thousands of burgers and hot dogs over the course of the next two days and nights.

"This is amazing," she said, turning to Chase. "You really get the sense that these guys have done this before."

"They have," Chase assured her. "This is the biggest base in Afghanistan, and hundreds of performers come through here. C'mon, I'll show you where your client will be able to relax when she's waiting to go onstage."

He took her elbow in a gesture that should have been impersonal, but Kate couldn't prevent herself from stiffening at the contact, and then pulling her arm away. She heard Chase mutter a curse and sensed that he wanted to confront her, but there was no way she could let him do that. She didn't feel strong enough to get into it with him about Captain Larson, and she absolutely did not want him to see how much it hurt her that he could go from her bed to another woman's bed.

Ignoring his frustration, she took her time examining the stage and the equipment preparations. She had been around concert performances for most of her life, first with her mother and then with Tenley. Watching the setup was as natural to her as breathing. When she had seen enough, she followed Chase into the building directly behind the stage. The USO had converted a dining facility into a large lounge area, with sofas and food stations, and just about everything the performers could want to either relax or practice before going onstage. There were several small rooms off to the side where they could even catch a quick nap.

Chase came to stand beside her. "The USO has arranged to have massage chairs set up for the performers, and there are some rooms in the back where they can warm up, if they choose to."

Kate nodded, satisfied with everything she saw. "What time is the first performance?"

Chase pulled a small notepad out of a pocket on his camo pants and quickly scanned through it. "The first performance is tonight, but it's more of a warm-up, with each group only doing one or two songs. Tomorrow, two groups will each perform three sets during the Independence Day barbecue while the other groups do photo signings and meet and greets. The real show begins early tomorrow evening, with all the groups performing well into the night."

"So when will Tenley go onstage?"

"I don't have the order of the performances. If you'd like, we can talk to the USO. They'll have that information."

"I know where they're located," Kate said quickly. "You don't need to come with me."

Chase looked swiftly around, then caught Kate by the wrist and all but dragged her to one of the anterooms. He pushed her up against a wall and trapped her there with a hand on either side of her head. She would have to duck beneath his arm in order to escape, but she could see by the grim expression on his face that even if she succeeded, she wouldn't get very far.

"What the hell is going on, Kate? When I left you last night, everything seemed fine, and then this morning you begin treating me as if I'm a goddamned leper." His eyes flashed. "Have I done something to offend you? Tell me what it is, so I can least try to fix it."

Kate swallowed hard. She'd known he wouldn't let her behavior go unnoticed, but she hesitated to tell him why she was angry. Too many times, her relationships had ended because the guy she'd been involved with had chosen to leave. She'd had no choice and hadn't been given an opportunity to try to correct the issue. She found she couldn't do the same thing to Chase without giving him the satisfaction of an explanation. She knew from experience what that was like, and it sucked.

Raising her chin, she met his eyes squarely. She could see the frustration and concern in their green depths, and something else, too. Heat. He wanted to kiss her, and the knowledge both thrilled and infuriated her, providing her with the courage to speak.

"I saw you last night," she blurted. "On my way back from the women's showers."

He cocked his head and looked expectantly at her. "So…? Why didn't you let me know? I thought we had an agreement that you wouldn't walk to the showers alone. You should have called me."

Kate compressed her lips and stared mutely at him, willing him to come clean with her, and not continue this farce of pretending he had no idea what she was talking about.

"I didn't call your name because it was clear to me that you were preoccupied with *kissing Captain Larson.*" She shoved angrily at his chest, but he didn't budge. "I saw you, Chase! I know you spent the night with her. The least you could have done is told me you were already involved with someone. Do you know how that makes me feel? Do you?"

To her astonishment, he didn't look guilty or ashamed at having been caught. In fact, his green eyes were alight with what might have been amusement and relief.

"Tell me how it made you feel," he said softly, crowding her with his body. "I want to know."

Kate couldn't believe he could be that cruel. His demand was equivalent to emotional torture. Lifting her chin, she glared at him.

"You want to know how it made me feel? Fine, let me tell you. It made me feel angry. And hurt. And stupid for having believed that you wanted me. And so mad that it took all my strength not to go in after you and scratch that woman's eyes out!" She stared at Chase, her breathing coming in aggravated gasps. "There, are you happy now? I wasn't even going to tell you that I saw you. I was just going to leave—go back to the States and pretend I never met you. But you—you—"

She made a sound of extreme frustration and tried to break free, but he clamped his hands on her upper arms and hauled her up against his chest.

"Katie," he said softly, searching her eyes, "do you really think I could so much as look at another woman after being with you? Do you really have such a low opinion of me?"

"I. Saw. You." The words came out through gritted teeth.

He considered her for a brief moment, then caught her by the hand and dragged her out of the room. "I want to show you something," he said over his shoulder. "Then, if you still want to hate me, you can."

Kate hung back, not wanting to go anywhere with him, but resistance was futile. He hauled her effortlessly in his wake across the parade field and back to the waiting Humvee. "No, wait!" she protested. "Where you taking me?"

"You'll see," he said grimly, and thrust her into the back seat, before climbing in beside her. "Take us to the flight-operations shack," he said, leaning forward to speak to the driver.

Kate stared at him in horror. "Oh, no," she said, reaching

for the door handle. "There is no way I am going to have a face-off with Captain Larson."

But Chase leaned across her body and covered her hand with his own before she could open the door and jump out. He searched her eyes, and what she saw in their depths made her pause. "Trust me, Kate, okay?" His voice was low and compelling. "Just give me this, and I promise I won't ask anything more from you."

Slowly, she released the door handle and sat back, still staring at him. "Okay," she muttered.

Satisfied, he resumed his position beside her, and they drove in silence across the base to the flight line. But instead of pulling up to the terminal, the Humvee drove to a separate building with a sign over the door that read Flight Operations.

Kate's heart was pounding so hard, she thought for sure that Chase must hear it, but he seemed too intent on getting her into the building to notice. Inside, three soldiers sat in a reception area, fielding phone calls and monitoring computers. The first soldier looked up, his gaze flicking from Chase to Kate, and then back again. If he thought it unusual that Chase was dragging a civilian female into the flight-operations center, he was too well-trained to let it show.

"The pilots are in the conference room," he said without preamble.

"Thanks," Chase muttered, and pulled Kate along a corridor until they reached a closed door. Without knocking, Chase opened it just enough to poke his head inside. "Sorry for the interruption. Can I speak with you privately? Now?"

Kate couldn't see who he directed his question to, but knew it was Captain Larson. Drawing a deep breath, she mentally steeled herself to face the pilot, vowing that she would never speak to Chase again for putting her through this humiliation. But it wasn't a female pilot who came out of the conference room.

Kate stared in dismay at the tall, broad-shouldered man who stepped into the corridor and closed the door carefully behind him. He wore an army-green flight suit with the US flag on one shoulder and an insignia patch on the other. Kate gaped at him, and her eyes dropped to the name patch on the front of his uniform. *Rawlins.*

"Oh, my God," she breathed.

She stared at him, registering the translucent green eyes, alight with interest, the square jaw and sensuous, smiling mouth and the deep dimples in each cheek. Like Chase's, his brown hair was cropped close to his head, and Kate could see the bronze and gold glints in the short strands. He was identical, in every way, to Chase. Except that where Chase's expression was grim and unsmiling, this man seemed to have a perpetual glint of devilment in his eyes. Now he looked from Kate to Chase.

"Ah," he said meaningfully and with great relish. "This has a distinct déjà vu feel to it."

"Kate," Chase said, "I'd like you to meet my brother—my *twin* brother—Chance Rawlins. He arrived yesterday morning from Bagram Air Base. He's an Apache helicopter pilot."

Chance gave her a winning smile. "I suspect that the reason you're here is because you saw me with a certain female pilot and mistakenly believed I was Chase."

Feeling light-headed, Kate threw out a hand to steady herself, but Chase was already there, putting an arm around her back and supporting her. "Are you okay?"

"I'm just…astonished," she finally admitted, leaning against Chase. "I had no idea…you said you had a brother, but you didn't tell me you were *twins.*" She passed a hand over her eyes. "I feel like such an idiot."

"Don't," Chance said, still grinning. "Not so long ago,

Jenna—Captain Larson—actually propositioned Chase, believing he was me. Don't worry, he turned her down. So this is all very cathartic for me. I don't often get to see my brother in this situation."

"Careful," Chase warned. He turned to Kate. "Are we okay? Are we good?"

Something loosened and then broke free in Kate's chest, and she felt her throat tighten with emotion. *Chase hadn't cheated on her.* Unable to speak, she just nodded.

"Okay, let's get out of here," he said. "Thanks for clearing things up, bro."

"My pleasure," Chance replied, his hand on the doorknob. "Oh, and don't forget my offer. Something tells me you're going to need it."

Chase steered her out of the building and over to the Humvee. "Are you sure you're okay?" he asked.

Kate looked up at him, not hiding anything. "I'm more than okay," she assured him, smiling. "I didn't get any sleep last night. I just kept replaying what I'd seen over and over again in my head until I thought I was going to lose my mind." She waved a hand dismissively. "I'm such an idiot, because it's not like I have any claim on you, right? You made it clear that you couldn't make any promises to me, and you're free to do what you want."

Chase frowned and blew out a hard breath. "Look, Kate, I said a lot of stupid things. When I said I couldn't do this, I only meant that it wouldn't be fair to ask you to wait for me. I hope you don't really believe that I'm capable of leaving your bed to climb in with another woman?"

It wouldn't be fair to ask you to wait for me.

The words reverberated through Kate's head. Had he really considered asking her to wait for him? Her heart lodged somewhere in her throat as she searched his eyes.

"No," she finally said. "I think you have more integrity and class than that."

He gave her a wry smile. "Thanks." He hesitated, and when he finally spoke, his words were carefully measured, but Kate didn't miss the intensity behind them. "Listen, I know this will probably seem crass, considering what you just went through, but Captain Larson is gone for the next few days and we've been offered a chance to use her housing unit. If you want to, that is. I could arrange for a security detail to watch over your sister, if that's a concern. But it's totally up to you, and I'll understand if you can't."

Just the thought of spending another night with Chase was enough to send her blood churning through her veins in anticipation. Did she want to be with him again? More than anything. Even the knowledge that they might not have any kind of relationship after she left Afghanistan wasn't enough to deter her. She didn't have the courage or the strength to refuse him. They only had these few remaining days together, and maybe she would never hear from Chase Rawlins again after that, but she was going to take whatever he had to offer and to hell with the consequences.

"Tenley will be jet-lagged and exhausted when she arrives," she finally said. "If I can get her to turn in early, then I'd like to take you up on that offer."

Chase grinned in relief, the dimples in his cheeks transforming his face so that Kate caught her breath, and she barely resisted reaching for him. "I'm glad," he said simply.

They both heard the roar of the jet at the same time, and turned to watch as an enormous plane approached the flight line, coming in on a steep spiral maneuver. Kate was certain the aircraft would slam into the ground. But at the last minute it leveled out and its wheels touched down on the runway, the engines throttling back as it screamed to a stop.

"Wow, that was pretty impressive," Kate said in admiration.

"You bet," Chase said. "Most flights make that combat landing. C'mon, let's get over to the flight line." He gave Kate a meaningful look. "Your sister is here."

13

Kate stood with Chase as the enormous aircraft taxied to a stop on the tarmac not far from them. Had it really been just three days ago that Kate had arrived at Bagram Air Base? She slid a sideways glance at the man standing beside her with his arms crossed over his chest, looking every inch the badass soldier that he was. She remembered how impressive he had seemed to her that first day, and how intimidated she had initially been by his don't-mess-with-me attitude. How would Tenley react to him? She was extremely sensitive and easily intimidated. Kate should have warned Chase.

"Listen," she said as an aside. "Tenley is very sweet and very friendly, but she might find you a little overwhelming. Be nice to her, okay?"

Chase slanted her an amused look. "Don't worry, I'll be on my best behavior. Relax, okay? Everything is going to be fine, you'll see."

Inwardly, Kate had her doubts, but she gave Chase a grateful smile, and then watched as the airplane stairs were rolled over to the side of the aircraft, and passengers began to disembark. At first, only uniformed soldiers made their way down the steps, but then several civilians appeared, wearing blue jeans and Western-style shirts. Kate recognized two of them as country music's biggest stars, and a cheer went up from the soldiers on the flight line. The musicians waved at the troops, and only the military police kept them from getting mobbed as they stepped off the stairs.

Kate stood straighter, hardly aware that she clutched Chase's sleeve. "Here they come," she said unnecessarily.

And then they saw her. Tenley's face appeared in the jetway, and she made her way carefully down the stairs. She wore her signature blue jeans and cowboy boots, and a white top with sparkling jewels around the neckline. Her blond hair hung in tousled waves around her face, and she carried her bubble-gum-pink guitar case in one hand. Hearing the cheers of the soldiers, she smiled brightly and raised a hand in greeting. The wind blew her hair around her face, and as she reached the bottom step, she tripped and fell, sprawling face-first on the tarmac with her hobo bag and guitar case in disarray around her.

Kate gasped and jumped forward, but Chase was already there, picking her up and crouching down to examine her knees and then her hands, before he scooped up her guitar and belongings. Tenley's face had turned a blotchy red, but she smiled and waved at the soldiers, and Kate could hear her telling Chase that she wasn't hurt. Seeing Kate, she smiled hugely and ran toward her.

"Oh, Tenley," cried Kate, reaching out and pulling the younger woman into an embrace. "Are you okay?"

"I'm fine," Tenley said, her voice muffled against Kate's shoulder. "Just embarrassed."

"Well, I'm so glad you made it here. I tried calling you to make sure you had the correct flight times, but you didn't answer." She pulled back and frowned at her sister. "Why didn't you answer?"

Tenley pulled free from Kate's arms, laughing. "I can't remember! Maybe I was over at the shelter. I've been trying to spend more time there, especially since they got a new shipment of dogs in."

Tenley loved animals, but believed her own hectic schedule didn't permit her to own a dog. Instead, she volunteered her spare time at a local rescue shelter. "Don't worry, Russell took good care of me."

"Well, you're here now," Kate said. She put an arm around the younger woman's shoulders and drew her toward Chase. "Tenley, you've already met Major Chase Rawlins. He's been my escort these past few days. He's going to look after us while we're here. We've been to three different bases, looking at the concert sites, and guess what?"

Tenley gave her an expectant look. "What?"

"I flew in a Black Hawk helicopter."

"Wow, that's amazing!" Tenley smiled, and then frowned. "What's a Black Hawk?"

"It's a military helicopter," Kate said, grinning at Chase over her sister's head. "Very cool."

Tenley turned to Chase. "Thank you for helping me back there. I'm sort of a klutz, so you'll have your work cut out for you in keeping me safe."

Chase inclined his head. "I'm up for the challenge, Ms. Miles."

"Oh, please call me Tenley." She turned to Kate. "Can we get out of here, please? I'm dying for a shower and a change of clothes." She made a face and put her hand over her nose. "What is that horrible smell?"

"That would be the Kandahar Riviera," Chase said, his dimples flashing.

Tenley turned to him in surprise. "They have a Riviera over here?"

"No, Tenley, they don't," Kate said patiently. "What you're smelling is the waste-treatment facility."

Her sister made a gagging noise. "It smells like rotten

onions. Do the poor soldiers who live here have to breathe that? I know this isn't the States, but surely we can provide them with clean air?"

"You get used to it," Chase said blandly. "Why don't I grab your luggage?"

"Okay, let's just go back to the housing unit so you can shower and eat and get some rest before tonight."

"What do you mean, tonight?" Tenley squeaked, a look of panic flitting across her face. "Please tell me I am not required to perform tonight. There's no way I can be ready to give a performance so soon!"

"Shh," Kate said soothingly, taking Tenley's guitar case from her and leading her toward the Humvee. "It's just one or two songs, not even a full set. Every group is performing tonight, just to get the troops in the mood."

"Are you sure they want me to?" Tenley asked, her voice anxious. "I think I heard a few soldiers booing me as I came off the plane. Why would they boo me?"

"Why do you think?" Kate asked calmly, putting her arm around Tenley's shoulders. "You insulted them. But that's why you're here—to show them that you didn't really mean what you said. Right?"

Tenley made a sound of distress. "I did mean what I said, just not toward all military. Just the ones who shipped Doug off."

Kate knew that if her sister ever discovered that she had been the one responsible for having Doug shipped overseas after their forced annulment, Tenley would never forgive her. She glanced over her shoulder to see Chase easily dismantling a pile of luggage in his search for Tenley's pink duffel bag. "So, listen…I told Major Rawlins that we're sisters…" She let her voice trail off.

Tenley pulled back to look at her. "You did?" Her voice registered her surprise. "I mean, that's great! If it were up to me, I'd tell everyone we're sisters, but I know you think it's better for my career if nobody knows we're related."

Kate nodded. "Right. But I'm not worried that Major Rawlins is going to alert the media."

Chase caught up with them, carrying an enormous pink duffel in one hand. He put it into the back of the Humvee and opened the door for Tenley and Kate.

"Wait," Tenley said, and glanced back toward the flight line. "What about the band members?"

"The USO is taking care of them," Kate assured her. "See? If you look over there, you'll see them getting on a USO bus. We'll have dinner with them later today."

Tenley looked in the direction Kate pointed, and a slight shudder ran through her slender frame. "Is that bus safe?"

"Don't worry," Kate said soothingly. "They're perfectly safe, and they only have a few miles to travel. In fact, we won't be too far from where they are. We have our own little trailer, just the two of us. Nice, right?"

"Absolutely," Tenley agreed, dragging her attention away from the bus and sliding into the Humvee. "I'm looking forward to it."

Chase held the door for Kate, and when their eyes met, he gave her a meaningful look. She wanted to kiss him for being so patient, but could only mouth the words thank you as she climbed in beside Tenley. He gave a philosophical shrug and a wink, and then closed the door firmly behind her before sliding into the front passenger seat.

"Oh, my God," Tenley moaned when they were underway. "I am so tired. How long before we're at our trailer?"

"We'll be there in less than fifteen minutes," Chase said over his shoulder.

But Tenley wasn't listening. She had pulled an iPhone out of her bag and was holding it at different angles, trying to get a signal.

"Don't even bother," Kate said drily. "There's no cell phone reception over here. Just put it away."

Tenley stared at Kate in disbelief. "Really?"

"Why don't you think of this as a little technology vacation?" Kate suggested, smiling. "You don't need to worry about any of that while you're here."

"Mmm, you're probably right. You always are. Ooh, my feet hurt." Tenley turned sideways on the seat, lifted her legs and plunked her feet in Kate's lap. "Take my boots off, Katie. I need a foot rub."

Giving Tenley foot massages was something that Kate had always done, but usually only after a performance, when her sister had been on her feet for several hours. She laughed. "Really? You want me to give you a foot rub right now?"

"Please?" Tenley stuck out her lower lip and gave Kate her sad-puppy face. "Pretty please?"

Kate sighed, acutely aware of Chase in the front seat, listening to everything. What must he think of Tenley, and of her for that matter?

"Fine," she relented. Grasping one boot by the toe and heel, she gave it a firm tug. "Pull, Tenley."

The boot came free, and Tenley wiggled her toes in bliss.

"Oh, that feels so good. Now the other one."

Kate dropped the boots on the floor and waved a hand under her nose. "Oh, man, are you sure about this? Your feet are…" She lowered her voice. "…sweaty."

"Sorry," Tenley said, sounding anything but. She waggled her toes in anticipation.

Taking a deep breath, Kate grasped her sister's foot and began to massage it, digging her thumbs into the arch until Tenley moaned with pleasure. "Oh, that feels so good! Oh, yes, harder. Deeper!"

In the rearview mirror, Kate saw the driver watching them, his eyes alight with masculine interest.

"Tenley," Kate admonished with an embarrassed laugh. "Keep it down." Glancing at the two men in the front seat, she dropped her voice to a whisper. "You sound like you're having an orgasm!"

"Right now, I'll take this over any orgasm," Tenley moaned, making no effort to lower her voice. "Any man would be lucky to have you, Kate, just for your foot massages."

Chase twisted in his seat until he met Kate's eyes, and she could see the amusement lurking in the green depths.

"Okay," she said firmly, pushing Tenley's feet aside. "We're done."

"Kate," she wailed. "You didn't even do my other foot!"

"And I won't if you continue to embarrass me," Kate hissed. "Honestly, Tenley, you're behaving like a child."

"Sorry," Tenley said, and sat up, searching for her boots.

"Here we are," Chase said as the Humvee drew to a stop outside the housing unit where Kate had slept the previous night.

Tenley pushed the door open and got out, staring at the unit. For a long moment, she didn't move or say anything, but Kate knew she was thinking about Doug and wondering if his accommodations were as luxurious as this modified trailer.

"This is where we're staying," Kate said brightly and linked her arm through Tenley's. "It's actually very cozy inside. Just wait until you see the accommodations at Camp Leatherneck."

Behind her, she heard Chase start to laugh.

THE SUN WAS BEGINNING TO SET, taking the worst of the day's heat with it, as the entertainment got underway. Kate had stayed backstage with Tenley until it was time for her to perform, listening as she moved among the other performers, chatting and laughing with them. She had a vibrancy that drew people effortlessly to her, and she seemed to thrive on the attention. Whereas she had been exhausted when she first arrived, now she seemed upbeat and excited.

Kate watched as Tenley took her guitar and stepped onto the stage and waved to a mixed reception of cheers and clapping and a smattering of boos. Kate walked over to Chase, who stood in the entry, and shrugged.

"Well, this is it," she said. "This is the reason we're here. Let's see how it goes."

"Are you kidding me?" Chase asked. "That girl is going to be fine. Look...they love her."

Kate laughed and together they made their way outside to stand at the edge of the parade field to watch Tenley perform. She silently acknowledged that Chase was right; the audience was cheering her sister's performance, the sound deafening.

"She sounds great," Chase commented.

Kate had to agree. Tenley strutted across the stage, stroking the strings on her guitar and swinging her blond hair around. Her voice was strong and pure, and she belted out the lyrics to her top hit with confidence. She wore a pair of white jeans and boots, paired with a blue corset adorned with sparkling stars. Against the backdrop of the American flag, she looked like every soldier's fantasy of the gorgeous girl next door.

"She's just so beautiful," Kate said wistfully, watching her.

"I agree," Chase said, but when Kate turned to him, he was looking at her, not Tenley.

"At least she didn't get my freckles...I inherited those from my father," she said, self-conscious. "When I was young, I would have given anything to have skin like Tenley's."

"Really? I love your freckles."

Kate gave him a disbelieving look. "You're kidding."

Uncaring of who might be watching, Chase stepped closer and traced a fingertip over her cheek. "I'm not kidding. A face without freckles is like a night sky without stars."

He shifted his gaze to hers, and for a moment Kate couldn't breathe. Without conscious thought, she leaned toward him, her lips parting.

A sudden commotion snapped Chase's attention away from her, and Kate turned to see what was happening.

A young soldier had pushed his way to the front of the crowd, avoiding the security guards, and pulled himself onto the stage. Kate stiffened and then sprang forward, but Chase was already moving, sprinting backstage to gain quicker access to the stage and intercept the soldier. At first, Tenley didn't realize the young man was right behind her, but when she turned around and saw him, her fingers slipped on the guitar strings, and the amplifiers made an earsplitting screech.

She stared at him for a split second, and then he stepped forward and took her by the arms. His lips were moving urgently, but Kate couldn't hear what he was saying. She could only see the look of disbelief on Tenley's face. Then Chase was there, yanking the soldier away from Tenley even as the security detail leaped onto the stage.

As Kate watched, the soldier stopped struggling and allowed Chase to escort him backstage. Tenley stood there for a moment, clearly shaken, but when her band picked up the strains of her interrupted song, she rallied. Clearly it was an effort for her to continue with the performance, but she managed to get through the number without any more incidents.

As soon as she finished, the crowd erupted into applause and cheering, and Tenley waved before jogging backstage. Kate met her there, anxious to see for herself that she was okay. There was no sign of either Chase or the young soldier who had attacked Tenley.

"Are you okay?" Kate asked, framing Tenley's face in her hands and searching her eyes.

"Yes, I think so," Tenley replied, but she seemed shaken by the incident. "He just surprised me, is all."

"What did he say to you?"

Tenley looked distracted, and her eyes were unfocused. Kate repeated the question.

"What?" Tenley shifted her attention back to Kate. "I, um, can't remember what he said. Everything happened so fast, and it was so loud up there that I couldn't really hear him that well."

There was no more opportunity to ask questions as Tenley's band members surrounded her, wanting to know what had happened. Kate hadn't gotten a good look at the soldier, but something about him had seemed vaguely familiar. She made her way back to Tenley.

"Did you know that young man?" she asked.

Tenley turned to her with a look of surprise, and then quickly seemed to compose herself. "No, of course not," she said quickly.

"Okay," Kate said. "I just thought…well, never mind."

Tenley shrugged and spun away, but Kate didn't miss how she chewed her finger, a sure sign that she was distressed. It was the same thing that Kate did when she was upset. "These guys all look exactly the same," Tenley said. "Same haircut, same uniform, same conformist mentality. He looked familiar to you because he looks like every other soldier."

Chase returned at that moment and approached Tenley. "Are you all right?" he asked.

"Yes, I'm fine," Tenley said, clearly exasperated. "What's going to happen to that soldier?"

"He'll be reprimanded, and probably banned from attending the rest of the Independence Day festivities."

Tenley frowned. "Please don't ban him on my account. I don't want him to get in trouble. I mean, it's not like he did anything really wrong. He just surprised me, that's all."

"We should put more security personnel around the stage," Kate said to Chase. "This is exactly why I asked that the troops be kept at least fifteen feet back from the stage. I don't want Tenley to have to go through this again."

"I agree," Chase said smoothly. "Why don't I escort you both back to your housing unit? I'm sure you're tired and it's probably a good idea to call it a night."

"No!" Tenley said quickly, then seeing Kate's surprised expression, she lowered her voice. "I mean, I'm not tired, and I don't want to go back to the housing unit. I'd like to hear the other performers."

Kate studied her sister. "Okay, if you're sure. Why don't I get you something to drink. Maybe a lemonade?"

Tenley gave her a grateful smile and sank into a nearby chair. "Thanks, that sounds great."

Chase fell into step beside her as she made her way to the food table. "Well, I understand why you feel so protective toward her. She does seem rather fragile and young."

Kate laughed. "Oh, no. Another country conquered by the fair Tenley. Russell says she's dumb like a fox."

"Who the hell is Russell?"

"Russell Wilson is Tenley's agent. He's the one who arranged for her to participate in this tour. He handles her concert tours, and I handle the rest. We're a good team, but sometimes he just doesn't understand Tenley."

"And I suppose he understands you?" Chase's voice was a low rumble.

Kate ordered a glass of lemonade and looked at Chase in surprise. "If I didn't know better, I'd think you were jealous."

"Damn straight," he said. "I'm jealous of any man who gets to spend time with you."

"Trust me, he has no interest in me," Kate said drily. "He's all about Tenley and the money she brings in."

She turned to take the lemonade to Tenley, but Chase stopped her with a hand on her shoulder. Kate looked at him expectantly, but his eyes were on Tenley. She had removed her white boots and was lounging back in her chair, laughing with one of the other performers.

"She's a great kid," Chase commented. "But I think she has you fooled, too."

Kate frowned. "What do you mean?"

He gestured to Tenley, who was now belting out an impromptu tune to the accompaniment of a guitar. "I think Tenley Miles can take care of herself. She's what…eighteen? She doesn't seem to have any trouble putting herself out there."

"Age is just a number," Kate said archly. "Tenley is a very young eighteen, and I'm in no hurry to push her out of the nest."

He raised an eyebrow, but she didn't miss the dimple that appeared briefly in one cheek. "I don't know if you've noticed, Kate, but she's already out and flying on her own. She's not a child anymore."

Kate frowned. No matter how successful Tenley might be, she couldn't stop thinking of her younger sister as a child. Maybe it had something to do with the fact that she wouldn't fully come into her inheritance until she was twenty-one. Both of her parents had been successful stars in their own right, and had left Tenley the bulk of their impressive estates, but she could not claim control of her fortune until her twenty-first birthday.

Chase was right. Legally, at least, she was an adult. But Kate cringed to think of Tenley trying to negotiate her way through life. She wouldn't be able to find her own way home from the corner coffee shop if Kate weren't there to guide her, and her soft heart left her vulnerable to those who would take unfair advantage of her.

Tenley chose that moment to set her guitar aside and walk toward them. "Hey, I hate to be a wet blanket, but I'm pretty beat. Must be the time difference."

"Are you ready to call it a night?" Kate asked in surprise, handing the lemonade to her sister. "I thought you wanted to stay and hear the remaining groups play."

Tenley yawned hugely. "I do, but I don't think I can keep my eyes open for another minute. But I don't want to ruin your night. If you don't mind walking me to the trailer, I'll be fine on my own and you two can come back and enjoy the rest of the festivities."

Chase gave Kate a meaningful look and she knew he was thinking about Captain Larson's empty CHU.

"Okay," she said, too quickly. "I mean, if you're sure…"

"Oh, I am," Tenley said. "I am completely exhausted."

"I'll drive you back," Chase offered.

"Where is the rest of my band staying?" Tenley asked.

"They have a large tent not far from here," Kate told her.

"A tent?" Tenley squeaked as she followed them to the Humvee. "Are you serious?"

"Well, it's more like a big fest tent," Kate explained. "Don't worry, they'll be very comfortable."

"If you're sure," Tenley replied. "I hate to think of them roughing it."

"Once they're asleep, it won't matter where they are," Kate assured her. "C'mon."

Twenty minutes later, Kate slipped out of the housing unit and Chase materialized from the nearby shadows. "How is she?" he asked.

Kate smiled. "Exhausted, but too keyed up to relax. I

gave her a mild sleeping tablet, so she should be out until morning."

"Did you give her the beeper?"

"Yes. I showed her how to use it and left it on the bed-side table."

"We'll be less than five minutes away if she needs us. But she won't."

They walked along the street without touching, although Kate was acutely aware of every movement he made. She could hardly believe she was going to do this—sneak away in the night to be with Chase. She felt as young as Tenley.

"Having second thoughts?" he asked quietly.

"Absolutely not," she said, flashing him a quick smile. "Just a little nervous. How about you?"

He laughed softly. "Nervous? Not on your life. It's been the single thing on my mind all day."

"Well then," Kate said, grabbing his hand and breaking into a light jog. "We should hurry. I'd hate to disappoint you."

14

"DARLIN," HE GROANED, "I don't know how you could think you could ever disappoint me. I mean, look at you."

They had reached Captain Larson's housing unit, and Chase had gotten them both inside without anyone seeing them. He turned on a small light next to the bed, and then took his bandana and laid it across the top of the lampshade to create a soft, muted glow.

As soon as he'd finished that, he'd turned to Kate and caught her hands in his, spreading her arms wide so that he could look his fill. Kate tried not to feel self-conscious, but couldn't help wishing that she had something more feminine and attractive to wear instead of her cargo pants and soft jersey top.

But Chase didn't seem to notice or care.

"Come here," he said roughly, and pulled her into his arms, hugging her tightly against his hard body. "You have no idea the hell I went through this morning when you gave me the frost treatment."

Kate tipped her head back and let her gaze drift over his features, committing them to memory. She traced the contours of his lean cheeks and square jaw, before she bracketed his face in both hands and drew his head down for a kiss.

"You don't know the hell I went through when I thought you had spent the night with Captain Larson," she murmured against his mouth. "I hope I never have to go through anything like that again."

With a groan, Chase deepened the kiss, sliding his tongue against hers and feasting on her mouth. Kate's blood began to hum through her veins, and she wove her fingers through his hair, loving the velvet-rough sensation against her palms. He smoothed his hand down over her hips and cupped her rear, pulling her up against his arousal.

When he released her and stepped back, Kate blinked. "What's wrong?" she asked.

"Absolutely nothing. But I want tonight to be special. And I've dreamed of undressing you, slowly, revealing you inch by inch." So saying, he reached out and unfastened the top button of her blouse, and then the next one, folding the fabric back and bending his head to press a kiss against the exposed skin. By the time he got to the last button, he was crouched in front of her, holding her hips in his big palms as he dragged his lips over her stomach. Kate ran her hands over his head, encouraging him.

"You're so soft," he muttered, and his fingers went to the fastening of her jeans. He drew the zipper down slowly, pushing the material aside and pressing his face into the open V, breathing deeply before kissing her through the silky fabric of her panties. "You smell good enough to eat."

True to his word, he undressed her slowly, pulling her pants free of her legs, and easing her blouse off until she stood in front of him wearing nothing more than her bra and panties. Standing up, he held her arms out and the heat and masculine appreciation in his eyes gave Kate a sense of feminine power.

Smoothing her hands over her stomach, she reached up and skated her fingers over her breasts before reaching behind her to unfasten her bra. Chase swallowed hard and she saw a muscle flex in his lean cheek.

"Do you want me to take this off, or would you rather do it?" she asked, tipping her head and giving him a sultry smile.

"No. I mean, I want to watch you take it off," he said, his voice husky.

Kate was amazed at how quickly and easily the tables had turned. She'd thought that he would pounce on her the second the door was shut; that he would consume her and possess her before she even knew what had happened. But he'd taken his time, and he'd made the mistake of letting her wield her power over him. She liked that feeling, and she wanted to keep it going.

Slowly, without taking her eyes from him, she slid the straps of her bra down her arms, letting the cups catch on the tips of her breasts until, finally, she let the garment drop to the floor. Chase released his breath on a soft groan, but when he would have reached for her, she held up a hand to forestall him.

"Not yet." She smiled. "You wanted to take this slow, so that's what we're going to do. Right now, all you get to do is watch."

Hooking her thumbs in the lacy waistband of her panties, she shimmied them over her hips and let them slide down the length of her legs until she was able to kick them free. She watched as Chase's eyes darkened with desire, and she could see the evidence of his arousal beneath his camo pants. Emboldened, she skimmed her fingertips over her breasts and stomach, and down to the apex of her thighs, wanting to tease him just a little.

"Kate," he warned in a soft growl. "You're killing me."

She felt no embarrassment at standing nude in front of Chase; the expression on his face told her clearly that he more than liked what he saw. But she wanted to do more than just arouse him; she wanted to completely rock his world and give him something to remember long after she was gone. Keeping that in mind, she walked slowly toward him.

"I don't want to do that," she assured him. "But I do want to kiss you."

Looping her arms around his neck, she allowed her breasts to brush against his chest, before she cupped his head in her hands and angled her mouth across his, licking along the seam of his lips until he gave an audible groan and opened beneath her onslaught. He tasted faintly of mint, and the sensation of his tongue sliding hotly against hers caused heat to slip beneath her skin until her entire body felt overheated and achy with need.

As she kissed him, her fingers worked the buttons of his camo shirt, and she tugged the hem free from his waistband. She slid her hands under the fabric, over the smooth, hard ridges of his abdomen. His skin was like hot silk, and dragging her mouth from his, she forged a path of moist kisses down his neck and over his chest, flicking her tongue against the small, flat nubs of his nipples.

He groaned, and when her fingers dropped to his belt and fumbled with the buckle, he brushed her hands away and unfastened it for her. Kate popped the button of his pants and slowly drew the zipper down. Chase's breathing was uneven now, but when Kate would have dropped to her knees, he caught her by the elbows and pulled her back up.

"What?" she asked. "I want to touch you."

"Ah, darlin', I want the same thing, but I don't want you on your knees." So saying, he backed her up until her legs encountered the edge of the bed and she sat down.

"Hmm," she said approvingly, now that his hips were at eye-level, "I like the way you think."

He looked incredibly sexy, with his camo shirt unbuttoned, revealing the corrugated muscles of abdomen, and Kate's mouth began to water. Chase's expression was taut as he watched her through heated eyes. Swallowing hard, she put her hand against him, feeling his hard length thrusting against her palm beneath the fabric of his pants.

"You're so hard," she breathed, glancing up at him.

A dimple appeared in one cheek. "You bet."

Kate pushed his pants over his hips, and slid her hand inside the waistband of his underwear. His breathing hitched as her fingers curled around him. Pushing his briefs down over his hips, she released him. He was long and thick, and the blunted head of his penis reminded her of a ripe plum. She wanted badly to taste him.

His hands stroked her hair as she bent forward and ran her tongue over him. He gave a loud groan, and his fingers traced the curve of her ears, but he didn't apply any pressure. Emboldened by his response, Kate took him in her mouth and swirled her tongue over his length, while she curled her fingers around the base and gently squeezed.

He tasted delicious, and she wanted more. With her free hand, she stroked his hip and buttock, and then cupped his balls, teasing him as she slid her mouth over him. His breathing was ragged now, and looking up at him, she saw he had put his head back. His eyes were closed and he looked like every decadent fantasy she had ever had, and her body responded instantly.

She increased the pressure and tempo of her mouth, until he began to thrust helplessly against her, and then pulled completely free.

"I can't last if you do that," he admitted raggedly, and bent down to unlace his boots and kick them off, and then push his underwear and pants free. Kate sat back and just stared. The guy was in amazing condition, and her fingers itched to explore the deep grooves of muscle that ran diagonally from his waist to his groin. Even his thighs were hard and muscled.

Peeling his shirt off, he bent down and slanted his mouth against Kate's as he pushed her back on the bed, licking and sucking at her tongue. His fingers kneaded her breasts as he kissed her. Sliding a hand behind one leg, he dragged it up and around his waist, and settled himself against the entrance to her body.

"I've been dying to do this," he muttered against her mouth. Easing himself to her side, he smoothed a hand over her stomach and dipped his fingers between her legs. Bending his head, he took a nipple into his mouth, sucking on it as he stroked her inner thighs, and then slid his fingers along her cleft until he found her center.

"Oh, man, you are so wet," he said against her skin. Kate cried out as his fingers tormented her clitoris, before he thrust a finger into her. "I want to watch you come."

Desire spiraled sharply through her, and her sex pulsed strongly around his finger. She felt hot and swollen and ached for release. Reaching for him, she wrapped her fingers around him and stroked his hard length, loving his grunts of pleasure. The torment of his fingers, combined with his sexy words, was too much.

"Oh," she gasped, feeling an orgasm building, "I'm going to…"

"Look at me," Chase demanded, slicking his fingers over her swollen flesh.

Kate did. His breathing was ragged, but his fingers never stopped working their magic. His green eyes were slumberous and seemed to glow with his arousal. Dipping his head, he licked her breast and then flicked his tongue against her nipple.

"C'mon, darlin'," he said hoarsely. "Come for me."

Kate did, and Chase caught her frantic cries with his

mouth as her hips bucked against his hand, flooding his fingers with her moisture. He didn't stop until he'd wrung every last shudder from her body, and she pushed weakly at his hand.

"Stop, please," she gasped, "I can't take any more."

Chase did, withdrawing his hand and pulling her against his chest. "That was amazing," he rasped against her temple. "Your entire body flushes when you have an orgasm. I could feel you tightening around my fingers, and you were so slippery."

Kate smiled and turned her face into his neck, embarrassed by his graphic description of her orgasm. Her muscles still thrummed with pleasure, and she reveled in the feel of Chase's warm body against hers. Reaching down, she ran the back of her fingers along his erection. He jerked against her, and when she stroked her thumb across the small slit, it came away slick with moisture.

"I can't believe I'm saying this, but I'm still aroused," she admitted, pressing a soft, moist kiss against his mouth. "I want to feel you inside me."

"Ah, babe," he growled softly. "You are so freaking sexy. Here, turn onto your stomach."

Kate did as he asked, bending her arms over her head. He straddled her legs and for a moment he just stood looking at her.

"You have a gorgeous back," he said, stroking his hands down the length of her spine. "And this, right here, where your hips flare out, is amazing." He cupped her buttocks and squeezed them, pulling them up and apart until she felt a sharp tug of arousal in her sex. He smoothed his hands over her buttocks, and then slid a hand between them to stroke her intimately from behind. "Oh, yeah, so wet...here, bend your knees."

He raised her hips up until her knees were bent and

splayed, and Kate knew he could see everything. Instead of feeling embarrassed, she grew even more aroused, knowing that this incredible man wanted her, and would soon take her with his own body.

He slid his hand over her, using a finger to part her. "Oh, man, if you could see what I'm seeing," he groaned. "You look amazing."

"I want you inside me," she said, sliding her hands beneath the pillow and arching her back even more. Turning her head, she watched as he looked at her. He had his thick cock in his hand and he gave it two quick strokes before he fitted himself against her entrance. His face was dark and flushed with arousal, his attention sharply focused on the spot where he entered her. Grasping her hip with one hand, he eased himself into her.

"You're so snug," he muttered. "Don't move."

He pushed further, and Kate moaned softly at the sensation of being stretched and filled. When he was finally fully inside her, he began to move, and Kate gasped with pleasure. The position and angle made him feel huge, and she welcomed how he grasped her hips and thrust strongly into her. He was long and hot, and the friction of his movement caused an answering heat to build inside her. She began to move against him, rotating her hips as he ground against her.

He moved completely over her, bracing his weight on one hand as he slid the other hand over her breasts, kneading them and tugging at her sensitized nipples. But when he slid his hand over her stomach and between her legs, lust exploded inside her. He stroked her clitoris as he filled her, and Kate cried out softly, feeling another orgasm begin to build.

"Oh, my God," she gasped, "you feel so good."

He grunted and swept her hair aside, kissing her neck and then swirling his tongue over her ear. "I want you to come again," he growled, and punctuated his words with another bone-melting thrust.

Kate was so close, but when he rubbed her hard, she came apart, crying out as she convulsed around him. She heard him give a deep, guttural groan, and then he surged into her one last time. He pulsed hotly inside her for several long seconds, holding her tightly, until finally, they both collapsed against the mattress.

"Oh, man," he said, withdrawing from her body and pulling her with him as he eased himself onto his side. "I think you killed me."

Trying to control her uneven breathing, Kate put her head on his shoulder and curled herself around him. Her body gave one last, convulsive shiver and Chase slid his arms around her, hugging her tight.

"That was…unbelievable," she said softly, and tipped her face up for his kiss.

Chase cupped her face in his hand and explored her mouth in a long, slow kiss that Kate felt all the way to her toes. When he finally pulled away, she thought he looked more content than she had ever seen him before. A smile played around his mouth and the lines of stress and fatigue were gone from around his eyes.

"I wish we could stay like this forever," she said, before she could stop herself.

He looked at her, sobering. "Yeah, me, too."

"I guess the military is going to want you back to do real work sooner or later."

"I guess so."

Kate raised herself on her elbow, propping her head on her hand as she studied him. She traced a finger around one of his nipples, and down the groove that bisected his body. "So why would they send someone like you to escort me around?"

"I'm with Special Ops, and the Pentagon issued a stand-down order the same day that you flew in. I was on a mission in northern Afghanistan when we got the order to return to base immediately." He gave a huff of laughter. "I was pretty irritated when I found out I was going to have to babysit a couple of entitled celebrities." He slanted her an apologetic look. "At least that's what I thought I was getting. Little did I know."

"And what did you get?" she asked, smiling.

"I got the sexiest woman I've ever known, and I think you care very much about your sister."

"Hmm. So if I'm hearing you correctly, you're not all that irritated anymore?"

Chase rolled over and pinned her beneath him, easily capturing her hands and holding them over her head. "No," he said, his eyes gleaming. "I trust my team to do their job until I return. In fact, I'll take great pleasure in showing you just how happy I am to be assigned to you…day and night."

He lowered his head and covered her mouth with his own, and Kate sighed in happy submission.

WHEN CHASE FINALLY walked Kate back to her own housing unit, it was almost 3:00 a.m. The roads were dark, and Chase used a small flashlight to illuminate their way. They didn't pass anyone, and when they reached the door to her unit, Chase took her in his arms and kissed her. After a long moment, he raised his head and gave her a rueful smile.

"I don't want to let you go, but you need to get some sleep. I'll come get you both for breakfast in about five hours, okay?"

Kate nodded, pressing her fingers against her lips as if she could still feel him there. She let herself quietly into her room and undressed without turning on the light. On the lower bunk next to hers, she could just make out the shape—

less lump of her sister, sleeping soundly. Easing herself into her own cot, she winced as the springs made a loud squeaking sound. But Tenley didn't move or make a noise, so Kate lay down and pulled the blankets over her shoulder.

She lay on her side for a long time, thinking about her time with Chase. She had no regrets. In fact, she couldn't remember when she'd last felt so happy. They hadn't talked about what would happen when she returned to the States, but Kate knew they could keep their relationship alive. Tennessee wasn't so far from North Carolina that they couldn't make it work.

Rolling onto her back, she looked over at Tenley's bed. She was brimming with so much inner excitement that she knew sleep would be an impossibility, and she wanted to share it with someone.

"Tenley!" she whispered. "Wake up." There was no sound from the other bunk, so she leaned over and shook the mattress. "Tenley!"

When there was still no response, Kate frowned and flipped on the small light. She stared in dismay at Tenley's empty bed. What she had thought was her sister was just the rumpled blankets and Tenley's backpack. Leaping out of her own bed, she quickly checked the top bunks, which were also empty. Her first panicked thought was that Tenley had been abducted. She recalled the young soldier who had jumped onto the stage. Had he somehow found out where Tenley slept? Checking the small side table, she found Chase's beeper exactly where she had left it earlier. Picking it up, she prepared to press the button when the doorknob of the housing unit opened, and Tenley entered.

"Oh, my God," she said, sagging in relief. "Where were you? I've been frantic!"

Tenley avoided her gaze. "Nowhere. I mean, I went to the bathroom."

"By yourself? I thought we talked about this. You aren't supposed to go anywhere without an escort."

Tenley gave Kate a helpless look. "Well, it wasn't like you were around to go with me. Where were you, anyway? And don't tell me the bathroom, because then I'd know you were lying."

"It doesn't matter where I was," Kate hedged. "You should have used the beeper like we agreed."

"I'm sorry," her sister said, sounding sincere. "I was tired and I really had to pee and I guess I forgot."

Kate drew in a deep breath and struggled for patience. "Okay. The important thing is that you're safe. Get some sleep."

She didn't miss how Tenley avoided her eyes as she sat on the edge of the bunk and kicked her shoes off. But as Kate waited for her sister to climb under the covers, Tenley flipped her hair back, inadvertently revealing a purplish bruise on her neck. Kate's fingers paused on the light switch.

"What the hell is that on your neck?"

Tenley at least had the grace to look embarrassed, and put a hand to the spot in an attempt to cover it. "It's nothing," she mumbled. "I've had it for a while."

"You have, my ass," Kate said, and reached over to pull Tenley's hair aside and inspect what was clearly a very large, very recent hickey. "How did you get this?"

"Stop it," Tenley said, pushing her hand away. "It's nothing."

"You didn't go to the bathroom," Kate accused. "You were with someone, and I want to know who it was."

"Yeah, right," Tenley retorted with uncharacteristic bitterness. "Like I'm going to tell you. Why don't we just share all our secrets? You can start by telling me who you were with tonight, as if I couldn't guess."

"What are you talking about?"

"I'm talking about your watchdog, Major Rawlins. The guy can't keep his eyes off you, and anyone can see he couldn't wait to get you alone. So I'm guessing that he succeeded, and that's where you've been all night. So leave me alone, okay?"

Kate felt herself go warm beneath Tenley's knowing regard. "The difference is that I'm an adult, Tenley, and I've at least had a chance to get to know Major Rawlins. You've been here for less than twenty-four hours and you've already hooked up with some stranger!"

Tenley climbed into her bunk and deliberately turned her back to Kate. "I don't want to talk to you about it," she said over her shoulder.

Kate tried one more time. "Tenley, you're a beautiful girl, but your status as a celebrity singer makes you a target. What do you really know about this guy?"

"I said," Tenley bit out, "that I don't want to talk about it."

Kate sighed, feeling more frustrated and confused than she had in a long time. She was losing Tenley, she could feel it. As she turned out the light and laid down, she recalled all the times Tenley had turned to her for advice. She'd been such a sweet, adorable little girl and Kate had loved looking after her. When had her baby sister become so grown up? When had she become capable of sneaking around behind her back?

Kate thought it had all started in Las Vegas, when Tenley had run off and gotten married to that soldier, Corporal Doug Armstrong. Believing him to be a gold-digger, Kate had moved quickly to have the marriage annulled. Then she'd made a few phone calls and had registered a complaint with his commanding officer. Within twenty-four hours, he had been shipped overseas.

Looking back, Kate knew she could have handled the entire situation differently, but she'd felt an enormous sense of responsibility toward Tenley. She couldn't let her sister ruin her life by getting married so young, and to a boy she barely knew. Thank goodness she'd been able to keep it a secret from the press, and even if Tenley's attitude had changed toward her, she had no regrets about what she'd done.

Curling on her side, she acknowledged that a chapter in her life was coming to an end. She would hang on to Tenley for as long as she could, but she knew, eventually, she would need to let her go. She only hoped she could.

15

THROUGHOUT THE NEXT DAY, Tenley made a point of avoiding Kate. She smiled and laughed at all the right times, and responded to her questions, but she made sure that Kate never had an opportunity to get her alone.

She and her band had performed two flawless sets, and the crowd had loved her. Afterwards, she posed, light-hearted and happy, for photos with the soldiers. She flirted with them and answered questions, and seemed genuinely interested in their comments. Over the course of the afternoon, she autographed dozens of glossy photos of herself without complaint. In fact, she smiled so brightly that Kate thought her face might split.

Music echoed across the base as each band took its turn entertaining the troops to thunderous applause and cheers. On the perimeter of the parade field, the food lines to the grills were hundreds of soldiers deep. Overhead, Kate noted several helicopters patrolling the skies, ensuring nothing happened to disrupt the festivities.

"She's doing a great job," Chase observed quietly as they watched Tenley pose with a group of young men. "How are you holding up?"

Kate hadn't had an opportunity to speak privately with

Chase until then. She wanted badly to touch him, and thrust her hands into her pockets. "When you walked me back last night, Tenley wasn't in her bed."

Chase gave her a questioning look. "Where was she?"

"That's just it, I don't know. She claimed to have walked to the bathroom, but she had a huge hickey on her neck."

His eyebrows rose. "Maybe she got it before she came over here."

Kate shook her head. "No, she was definitely hiding something and refused to talk to me about it. She hooked up with someone last night, but I have no idea who. What a disaster," she moaned. "I should have been there. I should never have left her alone."

Chase frowned. "Kate, she's not a child. You can't watch over her every minute of every day."

"But don't you see? I don't even have the right to criticize her about her behavior, because my own hasn't been much better."

She watched as twin patches of color rode high on Chase's cheekbones and realized she had angered him. "So what are you saying?" he asked. "That our being together last night was a mistake? A disaster?"

She gave him a pleading look. "No, that's not what I'm saying. But it was irresponsible. I had a duty to watch out for Tenley, and I failed. I left her alone to satisfy my own needs, and look what happened!"

"What? What happened that's so terrible?" Chase demanded. "Look at her, Kate. She's absolutely fine. You're her sister, not her mother. She's old enough to make her own decisions." He swept her with a hard look. "And so are you."

Without another word, he turned and walked toward Tenley, moving through the crowds with an easy authority that had soldiers clearing a path for him. He stood by Tenley's

shoulder, an imposing bodyguard in case any of the young
men surrounding her decided to get too friendly.

Kate blew out her breath in frustration. But there was
a part of her that believed she *had* behaved recklessly last
night, and no matter how wonderful her time with Chase
had been, she'd left Tenley alone and vulnerable.

She spent the remainder of the afternoon on the perimeter of the festivities, keeping Tenley in sight but not speaking with her. Chase had apparently made it his mission to
watch over her, and was never more than a couple of feet
from her side, his muscular arms crossed over his chest and
his face set in grim lines.

Kate chewed the side of her finger and watched them,
certain that in addition to losing Tenley, she may have lost
Chase as well.

FROM BEHIND HIS DARK SUNGLASSES, Chase watched Kate. She
looked lost and uncertain as she stood near one of the drink
stations, observing Tenley with a mixture of concern and
pride. More than anything, he wanted to go and reassure
her that everything would be fine, but her comments still
rankled. He sympathized with her, he really did, but only
because he sensed that Tenley meant more to her than she
would ever admit, maybe even to herself.

But he'd meant what he said. Tenley was legally an adult.
She had to take responsibility for her own actions. In the
end, it was her life, not Kate's.

Now he watched Tenley as she smiled and laughed with
the troops. She had a star-spangled bandana tied around her
neck, effectively hiding whatever mark Kate had seen. He
thought of the young man who had leaped onto the stage
the night before, and wondered if he had anything to do
with the love bites. The soldier had been silent and subdued
when questioned, and he'd refused to reveal why he had in-

terrupted Tenley's performance. All he would say was that he had something he needed to tell her and that it was for her ears only. The military police had decided the incident was nothing more than the exuberance of an overexcited fan, but Chase had his doubts. In the few seconds before he'd subdued the younger man, he had heard what he'd said to Tenley: *It meant something to me, too.*

Pulling out his BlackBerry, he sent an email to his team back at Bagram, requesting they send him an electronic version of Tenley's file. When he'd first received the dossier, he hadn't given it the same attention that he would have given the file of an enemy combatant or top Taliban leader. Now he kicked himself for his oversight. He'd been trained better than that. He knew better. He hoped the file might contain information that would give him some insight into both Tenley's and Kate's lives.

He smiled now as he watched Tenley pose for photos. He had to hand it to her; she had done a terrific job entertaining the troops. He glanced at his watch. The sun would be setting soon. One more group of performers was scheduled to play, and then the Independence Day celebration at Kandahar would be over. He would accompany Kate and Tenley to Camp Leatherneck in the morning, where they would do it all again before they flew to Bagram Air Base for the final performances.

Tenley caught his attention, waving him over with a smile.

"I'm so tired," she said when he bent his head to hear her over the crowd. "Can I go back to the trailer and take a nap?"

"Of course," he replied. "I'll walk you there myself." He waited while the USO representative made her excuses to the throngs of soldiers still hoping to get a photo or an autograph, and then walked with Tenley along the edge of the parade field, toward Kate.

"Have you talked with your sister today?" he asked.

Tenley shrugged, but Chase didn't miss the hot color that swept into her cheeks. "I've been busy."

Chase gave her a tolerant look. "She only has your best interests at heart. I think you know that. This is my fourth deployment to Afghanistan, and I've seen many, many performers come through here. But I have never seen a publicist care so much about her client's well-being that she would voluntarily come over in advance. By herself. Even if you are sisters."

But instead of showing gratitude, Tenley turned defensive. "That was her own decision," she said. "Nobody asked her to do it. That's just the way she is—a control freak."

"She obviously loves you a great deal. You might want to remember that."

"Just who are you supposed to be watching out for?" Tenley asked, slanting him an amused look. "Because if I didn't know better, I'd swear it was her."

They had reached Kate, who stood with her arms crossed, observing them. Now she smiled at Tenley. "That was a great performance."

"Thanks," Tenley said, not meeting her eyes. "I'm really tired so I asked Major Rawlins to walk me back to the trailer."

"I'll go with you," Kate said quickly, falling into step beside her. "I'm pretty tired, too."

"I'm not surprised," Tenley murmured, and looked meaningfully at Chase.

"Get some rest, Tenley," Chase said. "I'll come back in an hour or so, and if you're up for it, we can have someone drive us to the boardwalk to grab a bite to eat."

"The boardwalk?" asked Tenley. "That sounds almost civilized."

"We do our best," Chase said.

They reached the housing unit, and Chase stood aside as Tenley entered. Kate paused at the door and turned to look at him. He raised his chin and stared back at her, waiting.

"Chase," she began, "about last night—"

"Kate, I need you!" shrilled Tenley from inside the unit. "There's an enormous bug on the floor! You know how I hate bugs! Come and get rid of it!"

Kate frowned. "Be right there, Tenley." She looked at Chase and lowered her voice. "About last night…I don't regret any of it. I was where I should have been."

Chase felt something shift in his chest, and he didn't realize until that instant how much he had needed to hear those words. He didn't want her to regret anything about the previous night, not when it had been so perfect.

Not caring who might be watching, he stepped forward and hauled Kate into his arms. "If your light is on later, I'll knock," he murmured, and lowered his mouth to hers in a brief, hard kiss. "But first I'll get rid of your little pest so you can get some sleep."

"You mean Tenley?" she asked, smiling against his lips.

Chase chuckled and set her gently aside to step into the housing unit.

AFTER CHASE HAD CAPTURED and disposed of the harmless beetle, Kate changed into her pajamas and looked over at Tenley. "Do you want a cup of tea? That might help you sleep."

"Sure, but what I could really use are a couple of those sleeping tablets you wanted me to take last night. I feel too wound up after the concert to sleep."

"You mean the ones you didn't take?" Kate asked archly.

"I'll take them tonight," she promised, her eyes wide and innocent. "I really need to get some sleep."

Kate rummaged through her bag until she found the pills

and shook two into Tenley's palm. "Best take them with something to drink."

"How about having a cup of tea with me?"

"No, thanks. I'm not crazy about tea." Kate watched as Tenley turned on the kettle. In the next instant, she regretted her decision. She wasn't about to turn down what appeared to be a peace offering. "You know what? On second thought, I will have that cup of tea. Thanks."

She sat on the edge of her bunk and brushed out her hair, smiling her thanks as Tenley set her cup down on the bedside table.

"This is nice," Kate remarked. "It reminds me of the early days when I used to drive you all over the place to do auditions and gigs. Do you remember?"

Tenley smiled. "I remember. At least the hotels we stayed at were better than this place."

Kate blew on her hot tea and took a sip. "Well, just remember that most of the soldiers here don't have accommodations as good as these. Most of them are in tents."

They drank their tea in silence, until Kate yawned and put her cup down on the side table. "I guess I really do need that nap," she said. "I can barely keep my eyes open."

"Drink the rest of your tea," urged Tenley.

"No, I've had enough, but thanks." She grimaced. "I was never a big fan of tea and now I know why. It's too bitter." Sliding beneath the blankets, she bunched the pillow under her cheek and closed her eyes, sighing blissfully. "Turn out the light, Tens. I'm done."

A LOUD BANGING WOKE Kate from a deep sleep, and she pushed herself to a sitting position, groaning when she whacked her head on the underside of the top bunk. For a moment, she was disoriented, and scrabbled for the light, flicking it on and blinking in the sudden glare.

Someone was knocking on the door. Pushing back her blankets, she got to her feet and stumbled to answer it. Her head felt fuzzy and her mouth tasted terrible, like bitter tea.

"I'm coming," she called when the knocking persisted. Opening the door, she found Chase standing on her step. "What are you doing here?"

"I've been coming back every hour to check on you, but when your light never came on, I thought I should knock and make sure you're okay." His sharp gaze raked over her, missing nothing. "Are you? Okay?"

"Yes, of course," she said. "Just tired. What time is it?"

"Nearly 5:00 a.m. You've been sleeping for almost ten hours."

"What? That's impossible. I just lay down like ten minutes ago!" Whirling around, she checked Tenley's bunk, and let out a small wail of frustration. "I can't believe it! She's gone!"

Chase came into her quarters and closed the door behind him. Cupping her face in his hands, he searched her eyes. "Look at me," he commanded. "Your pupils are huge. Did you take a sleep aid?"

"No, I never take anything."

"Did Tenley take a sleep aid?"

"Yes, I gave her two..." Kate stopped speaking, as realization dawned. "Why, that little brat. She must have dumped those caplets into my tea! I wondered why she was being so nice, offering to make me a cup. And it tasted terrible."

"Well, my recommendation is to wait here until she comes back."

Kate stared at Chase in astonishment. "No, we have to find her. I want to know who she's with, Chase. We don't even know for sure that she's safe. We need to find her!"

Chase looked grim, and a muscle worked in one cheek. "Fine. But you may not like what you discover."

"As long as we find Tenley, I'll be happy."

Chase opened the door and gave a low whistle, and Charity trotted in, her tail wagging happily when she saw Kate. "Do you have something that Tenley wore recently? A shirt, maybe?"

Kate rummaged through Tenley's bag until she found the white jeans and top that her sister had worn to the concert earlier that day. "Will these do?"

"Perfect." Reaching into one of the deep pockets of his camo pants, he withdrew the dog's lead and snapped it onto her harness. Taking the clothing, he held it to Charity's nose. "Find."

Immediately, the dog began to sniff the room, and then turned to the door. Chase looked at Kate. "Put some shoes on and let's go."

"She can really smell Tenley?"

"You bet. She can scent a trail up to twenty-four hours after the subject has walked it."

Kate pulled on her shoes, still not convinced. "Even when her scent is mixed in with so many others?"

"A human loses up to forty thousand skin cells every minute," he said. "Those particles fall to the ground or get mixed in the air currents. A good tracking dog can distinguish the scent of your skin cells from those of another person."

Okay, maybe she was a little impressed. "I'm ready. Let's go."

Chase gave Charity a good thirty feet of lead, letting her set the pace. The dog moved quickly, her tail wagging happily. They passed the other housing units and turned down several small alleys, until they found themselves back on the parade field.

"Where is she taking us?" Kate asked.

"Looks like she wants to go to the building behind the stage," Chase replied.

They followed Charity through the door of the dark building, and into the large room that had served as a lounge for the performers. Chase flicked his flashlight around the room, but it was empty. The dog gave a whine and strained at the leash.

"She wants to go to that anteroom," Chase said, pulling the dog back toward him. "Wait here while I check it out."

"Not on your life," Kate muttered.

Chase wrapped the excess leash around his fist and allowed Charity to lead them to a closed door on the far side of the room. With a warning look at Kate, he put his hand on the doorknob and pushed it open, flashing his light into the dim interior.

Kate heard a startled shriek, and then Chase reached inside and flipped the overhead light on. "She's here," he said unnecessarily, stepping back so that Kate could push past him.

Kate stared in disbelief at the sight of her sister curled up on a cot with the young man who had jumped onto the stage the day before. Both of them scrambled to cover their nudity, and Kate looked quickly away.

"What are you doing?" she demanded.

"Kate!" wailed Tenley. "Why can't you ever leave me alone?"

Kate could hear both of them getting dressed. Chase stood just outside the door with his eyes straight ahead, and it wasn't until Tenley walked out of the room that he turned, his attention going to the young man who stood defiantly just inside the room.

"How many sleeping pills did you put in my tea?" Kate asked.

"I gave you four," Tenley admitted, keeping her eyes on the ground. "Just enough to make you sleep through the night."

"Don't blame Tenley," the young soldier said quickly. "None of this is her fault. I made her do it!"

"I hope for your own sake that's not true," Chase growled.

"Be quiet, Doug," Tenley snapped. "Let me handle this."

Doug. Kate refocused her attention on the young man, recognition flooding back. He was the same young soldier that Tenley had eloped with.

"You," she said, advancing slowly on him. "It was bad enough that you seduced my sister, but to have the nerve to—"

"Stop it!" Tenley shouted, and stepped between Kate and the young soldier. "I love him!"

"Love him?" Kate exclaimed in disbelief. "You hardly know him!" She directed her gaze to the man who stood behind Tenley. "It wasn't enough that you nearly ruined her life. Now you just can't leave her alone. How did you know she was going to be here?"

"I've never stopped loving her," he said fiercely. "I had no idea she was going to be here until I saw her up on that stage. You may have succeeded in having our marriage annulled, but you can't stop us from being together."

Kate turned to Chase. "I want this man arrested."

Chase was looking at Kate as though he had no idea who she was. "You had their marriage annulled?"

"We met during one of my concerts in Las Vegas," Tenley said. "Doug had scored a backstage pass, and as soon as I met him, something clicked. I knew he was the one."

Kate made a scoffing noise. "How could you possibly know that after thirty minutes with him?"

"It was an entire night, Kate!" Tenley shouted. "You were too busy talking on the phone and promoting my next tour to even know what I was doing. You didn't even know I was gone until the next morning." She turned to Chase. "Why don't you ask Kate what happened after she tracked us down and had our marriage annulled?"

"Tenley," Kate protested, her voice weak. "Don't."

Ignoring her, Tenley leaned forward until her face was mere inches from Kate's. "The military shipped him off to Afghanistan! We were in love, Kate, and you tore us apart without a second thought. You didn't even ask me how I felt! They shipped him off to the other side of the world, and because of your restraining order, I couldn't even find out where he was sent."

"You're little more than a child!" Kate argued. "You barely know him! And it's impossible to fall in love that quickly. This isn't some romantic remake of Romeo and Juliet, this is real life!"

"I'm not a child," Tenley asserted, drawing herself up. Stepping back, she put her arms around Doug. "I love him, and I'm going to marry him. Again."

Kate put a hand to her forehead. "I don't believe this. Tenley, think about what you're doing. Come back with me now and we can at least talk about it. I mean, what do you really know about him? You haven't been with him long enough to know if you love him."

Tenley's glance flicked between Kate and Chase. "Maybe *you* need more than a few days to decide if you love someone," she said, "but not me."

"Tenley—"

"I can't do this anymore, Kate." Tenley looked at her imploringly. "I need to make my own decisions, not have you make them for me."

"Please—"

"You're fired, Kate. I don't want you as my publicist or my personal assistant. In fact, as soon as we get home, I'm finding my own place to live."

Kate stared at her, unable to comprehend what was happening. "What? No! Don't do this, Tenley."

"Don't you see?" Tenley asked, her voice softening. "I have to. I can't let you make all my decisions for me. Not anymore. What's right for you isn't necessarily right for me. That's why I have to do this, Kate."

Kate took a step back, stunned. She would have stumbled if not for Chase's strong arm supporting her.

"C'mon," he said quietly. "I'll walk you back." He pinioned the young soldier with a hard look. "I want Tenley returned to her housing unit within thirty minutes, Corporal. If she's not there, you'll answer to me. Are we clear?"

Doug nodded. "Yes, sir. Thank you, sir."

"C'mon, Kate," Chase said, putting an arm around her shoulders and leading her out of the building. "I'll make sure she gets back safely. Let's get you some coffee and then we can figure this thing out."

She nodded and let him hug her as they walked, too stunned to argue. Surely she was still asleep and this was all just a bad dream. Right now, Chase was the only sure thing in her life, but if Tenley had really meant what she said, then he was also the next person she would need to say goodbye to. Because if Tenley didn't want to work with her, then she would not be traveling to the other bases; she would be on the next flight back to the States.

Her chest ached at the thought of leaving Chase, but she recalled what she had said to Tenley with such great authority: *You only knew him for a few days! It's impossible to fall in love that quickly.*

Did she love Chase? She didn't know. But she did know one thing; she wasn't going to make the same mistake her sister had.

16

CHASE COULDN'T EVER RECALL feeling such a strong protective instinct toward anyone as he did now with Kate. He'd seen the stricken expression on her face when Tenley had told her she was fired. Knowing how much Kate had sacrificed for her sister, he could only imagine what she was going through.

He took her back to Captain Larson's housing unit and made her a strong cup of coffee in an effort to combat the residual effects of the sleeping pills. She sat curled up on the small sofa, her hands cupped around the mug as she told him stories of how she had raised Tenley after she was orphaned. Kate had been little more than a child herself at the time, barely the same age as Tenley was now. His heart ached for her. It had to have been difficult, no matter how perfect she tried to make it sound. Knowing Kate, she'd tried to provide Tenley with the perfect childhood that she herself had been denied, even at the cost of her own dreams.

For the first time, Chase understood the enormity of what Kate had sacrificed for her sister, and also what she had just lost. He crouched in front of her and gently took the cup of coffee from her hands and set it down, curling his own hands around hers.

"Listen, Kate," he began, "I think if you give Tenley some time, she'll come around. She loves you, and I know she doesn't want to hurt you. But maybe some space between the two of you isn't such a bad thing."

Kate smiled ruefully. "I guess I didn't want to admit that she was all grown up. I wanted to hang on to her for as long as I could. But still, to *fire* me?"

"Maybe she'll reconsider."

To his surprise, Kate laughed. "That's not possible. You see, I didn't get paid for what I did. She never actually hired me. I just sort of assumed the role of personal assistant because we didn't want to publicize the fact that she was being raised by a sibling, and not some court-appointed guardian, like the media believed. So technically, I never actually worked for her."

Chase frowned. "You did all that for her without getting paid? How do you get by? Pay your bills?"

"I have a small trust fund that I use for expenses." She shrugged. "But I do a little web-design work on the side that provides me with pin money."

"You're a web designer?" He couldn't keep the astonishment out of his voice.

"Well, I *wanted* to be a web designer," she clarified. "I attended three years of night school to become a webmaster, but dropped out when Tenley was nine years old, because it was clear even then that she had talent. But I did design her website, and a few others, too. They've even won awards. I was hoping I'd be a lot closer to starting my own business by now, but Tenley's career has kept me too busy for much else."

"I'm impressed." He was. And happy to know that she had something she could focus on besides Tenley. "Maybe this is your chance to get your web-design business up and running."

She made a face. "I don't know. Maybe."

Chase looked down at their linked hands and gathered his courage. He'd never felt so uncertain, even when he'd been on a dangerous mission with no idea if it would end well, or badly.

"Here's the thing," he finally said. "I have to be here for another six months, but I want us to stay in touch. More than stay in touch, actually." He looked up at her. "I want you to wait for me, Kate."

Her lips parted on a soft *"oh"* of surprise. "Wait for you? As in *wait for you?* What are you saying?"

He gave a self-conscious laugh and peered up at her. "You really don't know? I'm saying that I want an exclusive relationship. We can video-chat with each other whenever I'm on a base. And when I get back, I'll return to Fort Bragg. That's about ten hours from Nashville, but we could make it work."

Kate stared at him in bemusement, until finally she pulled her hands away and stood up. "This is all moving too fast," she murmured.

Chase dipped his head to look into her eyes. "We can go as slow as you want, darlin'. I just need to know if you'll wait for me."

He'd surprised her. He could see it in her eyes. "You hardly know me," she said softly.

Chase struggled to keep his voice low and patient. "Then let's take the next six months and get to know each other the old-fashioned way. We'll talk and send letters, and when I get back, we'll go away somewhere, just the two of us. Did I tell you that I have a little place on the beach in Beaufort?"

Kate smiled. "Chase, you make it all sound so lovely, but I can't make any decisions right now. I've just lost the only job I've ever had—"

"Which is a good thing," Chase enthused. "You can do web design anywhere. Come to North Carolina. You'll love it, I promise."

He understood that her life had just been turned upside down, but there was no way he was going to let her run away to lick her wounds. He wanted to give her something to hope for, to look forward to. He wanted to give her a new start, with him at her side.

"What if you change your mind?" she asked, searching his eyes. "Six months is a long time. What if I come down to North Carolina and you realize you made a mistake? What if you no longer find me attractive?"

Chase laughed softly and cupped her face in his hands. "That is not going to happen. Don't you get it? I'm crazy about you." He lowered his head and covered her mouth in a slow, sweet kiss designed to show her just what she meant to him. When he finally pulled away, he was gratified to see her eyes had gone hazy with pleasure. "Have I convinced you yet?"

She leaned into him with a soft sigh, her hands curling around his shoulders. "Not quite. I may need a little more persuasion."

"With pleasure," he rumbled softly, taking her fully into his arms. "If it's okay with you, I'm going to spend the next few hours persuading you."

He heard her breath catch, and his own quickened at the sensual promise in her eyes. "Then I won't tell you how gullible I am, or that I have no willpower to resist you," she said breathlessly.

Chase chuckled. "I'll take that as a *yes*."

CHASE PICKED HER UP the following morning before dawn, having secured a seat for her on a flight to Kuwait. From there, she would fly to Atlanta, and make her way home to Nashville. He had walked her back to her housing unit before dawn, but she hadn't gone to bed, too consumed with thoughts of Chase to sleep. For the first time that she could recall, she was filled with a sense of hope and excitement.

She couldn't even feel remorse over the fact that Tenley had fired her, because in doing so she'd opened up end- less opportunities for Kate. And while she hadn't verbally agreed to relocate to North Carolina, she'd let Chase do his best to persuade her.

Now she watched as he stowed her duffel bag in the back of the Humvee. Charity sat in the backseat and her tail thumped happily as Kate reached over to rub her head. "I am going to miss you," she said, stroking the dog's ears.

Chase grunted as he climbed into the front seat beside Kate. "I can't believe I'm jealous of that mutt."

"I'm going to miss you, too," she said, letting her gaze travel over his face, memorizing his features.

He turned toward her in his seat. "I'll call you as often as I can, but I don't want you to worry if several weeks go by without hearing from me."

She took a deep breath and laced her fingers with his. "I know you'll be careful."

"You bet."

Too soon, they arrived at the terminal. Kate's flight wasn't due to depart for another three hours, but passengers were required to arrive early. Even at this hour, the lobby was filled with soldiers waiting to catch a flight, and military duffel bags and gear littered the floor. As they made their way through the lobby to the check-in line, Kate grabbed his sleeve and pulled him to a stop.

"Look," she breathed, staring at one of the flat-screen televisions mounted on the wall.

Chase followed her gaze and felt his stomach drop. There, on national television, was a video of Tenley Miles locked in a passionate embrace with a uniformed soldier backstage at the Kandahar concert. The crawl line across the bottom of the screen read, Beyond the Call of Duty?

Kate turned to him. "Chase, I need to see Tenley. She's not going to know how to handle this. She needs me to do damage control!"

"Kate," he said warningly.

"I have to do this," she insisted. "Just last week she was ripping the military apart, and now she's caught kissing some soldier? You and I know the truth, but the media is going to have a field day, never mind the embarrassment this will cause for the Army!"

She knew the instant he realized she was right. "Fine," he bit out. "Let's go. But just for the record, I'm all for letting her handle this one on her own."

They drove over to the tent where the performers were sleeping, but Tenley was already awake and sitting outside at a picnic table, sharing a cup of coffee with Doug. Kate had to admit that the two made an attractive couple.

"I'll tell her," Kate said to Chase as she grabbed the door handle.

Chase put his hands in the air. "Absolutely. You'll get no argument from me on that."

Kate didn't miss the way Tenley stiffened when she saw her.

"Tenley, I need to talk to you," Kate said without preamble, sitting down next to her sister. "I just saw a video clip of you and—and Doug on television. You were caught on camera kissing backstage. The media is going to have a field day with this, but I think I have a way that we could explain it and make the public sympathize with you."

Tenley's face had gone pale, but now she reached over and covered Doug's hand with her own, smiling in a way that Kate had never seen before.

"Kate," she said gently, "you're not my publicist anymore. This isn't your problem to handle."

"But you're still my sister." Kate frowned. "And whatever you might think of me, I know how to work the media. I can fix this, Tenley."

"Nothing needs to be fixed," Tenley insisted. "I don't care if the whole world knows I was kissing Doug backstage. I love him. I'm going to be honest and tell the press that Doug and I met and fell in love in Las Vegas last month. There's a reason I came to Afghanistan, Kate. I didn't plan for this to happen, but now that we've found each other again, I'm not letting go." She gave Kate a sympathetic look. "Don't worry. I know what I'm doing. And even if this backfires on me, I'm a big girl. I can accept the consequences, Kate."

Kate stared at her sister, barely able to believe what she was hearing. "Are you serious?"

Tenley leaned forward and gave her a hug. "I'm completely serious." Reaching out, she took Kate's hand between her own. "I know you're upset that I fired you, but I can't let you put your life on hold for me any longer."

Kate shook her head. "I haven't put my life on hold, Tens."

"Yes, you have. You think I don't know what you've given up for me? *Everything.* You left college to take care of me. I know you had dreams of starting your own web-design business, and instead you've given that up to take care of me. I love you, but I want to make my own choices, even if they're not always the right ones. I'm giving you back your life, Kate." Her gaze flicked to Chase, standing by the Humvee. "Don't waste it."

Kate returned her hug, watching Chase over her sister's shoulder. He had his cell phone pressed to his ear, oblivious to the momentous event that was unfolding at the picnic table.

She dragged her gaze away. "I'm proud of you, Tens, I really am," she said.

Tenley pulled away and looked at Kate. "I want you to stop worrying about me. I'll be fine." Reaching over, she grasped Doug's fingers. "I have Doug now."

Kate drew in a deep breath, realizing this was a new beginning for both of them. "Okay," she said, forcing a smile. "But you know how to reach me if you need me. If you're sure...I have a plane to catch."

For just an instant, an expression of doubt and regret flashed across Tenley's features. Then she looked at Doug and seemed to draw strength from his smile.

"Have a safe flight," she said to Kate, and hugged her again.

Reluctantly, Kate rose and walked back toward the Humvee. Chase was still talking on his cell phone. As she watched, he snapped it shut and Kate couldn't help but notice a new determination in his stride as he returned to the vehicle.

He slid into the driver's seat and turned the key. "Everything go okay?"

"Surprisingly, yes. I mean, Tenley isn't at all concerned about the publicity, and she seems to actually have a plan."

"That's a good thing, right?"

"Yes, I think it is. Who was that on the phone? It seemed like a pretty intense conversation."

Chase thrust the vehicle into Drive and they bounced along the uneven roads of the base, back toward the flight line. "The stand-down order for Special Ops has been lifted. By this time tomorrow, my team and I will be back in the field."

Kate stared at him and her heart seemed to skip a beat at the thought of him in danger. "So if you're returning to duty, who will travel with Tenley and the rest of the performers?"

Chase glanced over at her. "You have nothing to worry about, Kate. She'll be well taken care of."

She nodded. "I know. I guess some things are just harder to let go of."

His hands tightened on the steering wheel. "Tell me about it."

The remainder of the trip was made in silence, and Kate couldn't help but think that she was going home a very different person than she'd been when she had first arrived, just five days ago. She was leaving Tenley behind. She was leaving Chase behind.

She was leaving her heart behind.

They reached the terminal, and Chase hooked the lead to Charity and let her join them as they made their way through the lounge to the flight line. He waited while Kate checked in, and then walked outside with her. A bus was already there to take them across the tarmac to the plane.

"So I guess this is it," she said, smiling brightly at him. She had told herself a hundred times that she would not cry.

Chase reached into his breast pocket and pulled out a small card. "I want you to keep this close," he said. "Here is my address and the phone number for my headquarters offices, both here and at Fort Bragg. This is my email address, and on the back, I've written my stateside address and phone number. And just in case you can't reach me, I've included my brother's address."

Kate took the card and turned it over in her hands. "Thanks. I guess I don't have to give you my information, right?"

"I have your personal information," he confirmed, his eyes gleaming. "Do me a favor and let me know when you get home safely, okay?"

Kate nodded. "Okay."

"Come here," he said roughly, and hauled her into his

arms, uncaring of who might be watching. "You look after yourself. And call me if you need anything, got it?"

Kate nodded, feeling as if something in her chest was about to break. "I'll call you," she promised. Not wanting him to see how close to tears she was, she pulled free of his embrace and bent down to hug Charity. "What will happen to her?" she asked, burying her face in the dog's rough fur.

"I don't know," Chase admitted. "I haven't found anyone willing to sponsor her yet. But I'm not giving up. I still have six months."

"I'm sure it will all work out," Kate said, standing up.

Chase looked beyond her to the flight line. "Looks like your bus is boarding," he said.

With a small sob, Kate flung her arms around him and pressed a hard kiss against his mouth. Then, afraid of what she might do or say, she turned and walked swiftly toward the bus. She felt his eyes watching her the entire way, but she refused to look back. Only when she was on the bus did she finally allow herself to glance back where she had left him.

He was gone.

17

Six months later

CHASE DIRECTED THE taxi driver along the sandy road that paralleled the beach, his eyes scanning the street until his little beach cottage came into view. Had it really been more than a year since he'd been home? He drew in a deep breath, willing his heart to slow down. He couldn't recall the last time he'd been this nervous and excited all at the same time. Even when they'd finally managed to capture Al-Azir, in a mission that had challenged him on every level, he hadn't felt the way he did now.

Uncertain.

Optimistic.

Scared as hell.

He had four weeks of leave ahead of him before he needed to report back to Fort Bragg. He could have gone to Texas to spend time with his folks. Instead, he'd come directly from the airport to Beaufort, North Carolina, because that's where Kate was waiting for him. He hadn't even changed out of his uniform.

"Pull up here," he instructed the driver, peeling some bills from his wallet and handing them over.

Grabbing his gear from the trunk, he set everything down at the end of the walkway and took a minute just to look. The cottage was exactly as he remembered, with the overhanging porch and weathered shingles. Only now, flowering pots hung between the pillared supports and someone had put a fresh coat of paint on the door and windows. A small table and two chairs had been placed on the far end of the porch, where the view of the water was unobstructed.

He'd hoped to see Kate waiting for him on the porch, but maybe she was inside. Drawing another deep breath, he picked up his duffel bags and made his way to the door. It opened beneath his fingers, and he stepped into the house, knowing instinctively that he was alone.

Kate wasn't there.

His spirits dipped in disappointment.

Setting his gear down in the corner, he walked slowly through the rooms, his boots heavy on the wood floors. Everything was the same, yet different. He noted the subtle changes, like the floral rug in the living room that brightened the small space and drew his attention to the fresh flowers on the coffee table and on the fireplace mantel. In the kitchen, a pale green sweater lay draped over the back of a chair. Chase picked it up and carried it to his face, breathing in Kate's scent.

Where the hell was she?

After she'd left Afghanistan, he'd spent hours on the phone and online, persuading her to move to North Carolina and into his beach cottage. It made no sense for the house to sit empty when she could use it, he'd argued. There was a spare bedroom if she didn't feel comfortable sleeping in his bed. She could use the time to get her web-design business up and running, and if she wanted to find her own place after he returned, he wouldn't argue. She'd be doing him a favor by looking after the place for him.

In the end, she'd relented and he'd known a fierce sense
of satisfaction in picturing her there, in his house. Sitting on
his porch. Using his shower. Maybe even sleeping in his bed.

Walking down the hallway, he pushed open the door to
his bedroom, and gave a huff of disappointed laughter. Definitely not sleeping in his bed. Not yet, anyway. His room
was as Spartan as it had been when he had left it more than
a year ago. There were no traces of Kate here.

Closing the door, he continued down the hall to the next
room. What had been a sparsely furnished storage and guest
room was now a distinctly feminine bedroom. Gone were his
Texas Rangers bedspread and the stash of spare army gear
he'd kept piled in one corner. The bed now boasted a downy
comforter in a floral pattern, and at least a half dozen pil-
lows. More cut flowers stood on the nightstand and dresser,
and feminine underclothes lay strewn across the bed and on
a nearby chair. A dozen framed photos adorned the walls
and he stepped closer to inspect them, seeing they were pic-
tures of Kate and her sister, and even one of a very young
Willa Dean holding an infant.

A work table had been set up against one wall as a makeshift desk. A pile of books and papers surrounded Kate's
laptop, which sat open and blinking. Curious, he tapped
the keyboard and the monitor flared into life. He could see
she was in the middle of designing a website, and he bent
down for a closer look, impressed when he saw her client
was a top model.

Leaving her room, he went into the backyard. Flower
beds had been planted near the house, and a new set of out-
door furniture sat beneath a bright patio umbrella. Kate had
left a plate and a half-empty glass of lemonade on the table.
Chase was getting ready to carry them into the house when
he heard the crunch of gravel in the driveway.

He paused, listening. He heard one car door slam, and

then another, followed by the loud barking of an excited dog. Setting the dishes back on the table, he rounded the side of the house to the front yard. He didn't recognize the gray sedan parked in the driveway, and for a minute he didn't see anyone. But another excited bark drew his attention to the front porch. A woman stood with her arms around two bags of groceries, while a dog on a leash nearly pulled her off balance. Setting the bags down, she bent to try and quiet the animal, who leaped up and gave her face a happy lick.

Kate. And she had Charity with her.

His heart began to pound fast in his chest, and his first instinct was to bound up the stairs and grab her. Instead, he rubbed his palms against his thighs and walked to the bottom of the steps.

"Kate."

She whirled around, but before she could respond, Charity gave a yelp and lunged forward, leaping off the porch and yanking Kate with her. Chase reacted quickly, grabbing the dog and the leash, and extending an arm to catch Kate as she pitched down the steps, the bags of groceries falling out of her arms and spilling across the walkway. She clutched at his shoulders, laughing, as Charity squirmed with delight and tried to lick him anywhere she could reach.

Keeping an arm around Kate, he crouched down to greet the dog, rubbing her head and ears, and murmuring words of affection to her. When she rolled onto her back, he scratched her belly and then, with a final pat, stood up and pulled Kate into his arms. She gazed up at him, her coffee-dark eyes filled with welcome and an enticing shyness.

"You're even more beautiful than I remembered," he said, his voice husky.

She flushed and looked down, and then determinedly lifted her chin and met his gaze. "Thank you. I was hoping to have dinner ready for you before you arrived."

He trailed the backs of his fingers along her cheekbone. "You think I'm hungry for food?" he growled softly, teasing her. But it took all of his self-restraint not to pick her up and carry her bodily into his bedroom. For six months he'd fantasized about this moment, but he wasn't going to ruin it by moving too fast.

Crouching, he scooped pasta and bread and fresh vegetables back into the bags. "How did you manage to bring Charity back?" he asked, reaching out to rub the dog's ears. He felt an unfamiliar tightening in his throat as he patted the animal. He'd thought he'd never see her again. "I left her with the K-9 unit three months ago, when I had to leave for a mission. When I came back, she was just gone. I was told her owner had come back to claim her."

Kate smiled and bent down to retrieve a tomato that had rolled into the grass. "I'm so sorry. I asked them not to tell you. I wanted to surprise you when you came home. Actually, it was Tenley who arranged it all," she said, on eye level with him. "She heard through Doug that one of the women from the USO was coming back to the States on a commercial flight. Tenley asked if she would be willing to escort Charity, and she said she would. We weren't sure if we'd have another opportunity like that one, so we just grabbed it."

Chase gave a disbelieving laugh. "Wow. That's amazing. So Tenley and Doug are still together?"

"They're married, for keeps this time. He came home about a month ago. She's taking some time off from touring, and so far they seem to be doing great."

"And you and Tenley…?"

"Also doing great," Kate assured him, rising to her feet. "In fact, it's amazing how our relationship has changed, now that I'm not trying to run her life. I finally have the sister I always wanted."

"And you and me…?" Chase stood up and threaded his fingers through her silky hair, studying the strands. "How are we doing?"

Kate stepped closer to him, her hands going to the front of his uniform, where she rubbed her fingers over his embroidered name tag. "Much better, now that you're home."

Home.

He couldn't believe how much promise that single word held. Cupping her face in his hands, Chase bent down and kissed her, putting everything he had into it and letting Kate know how he felt. When he finally raised his head, her eyes were shining with unshed tears. "I've missed you so much, Chase. I still can't believe this is real."

Chase smiled and tipped his forehead to hers. "What can't you believe?"

"All of this. You…being here…finally doing all the things I want to do."

"Oh, it's real," he assured her. "Let me show you."

Without giving her a chance to protest, he swept her into his arms and took the steps to his house two at a time, with Charity following close on his heels. Kate threw her arms around his neck and hung on tight, but he could feel her smiling against his neck. He didn't pause until he reached his bedroom, where he stopped in the doorway and looked down at the dog. She stared at him with hopeful eyes, her tail wagging.

"Sorry, girl," he said, leaving her in the hallway, "but this mission is all mine."

Turning toward the bed, he kicked the door closed behind him.

* * * * *